Desert Blooms

Book Two
Luce Velazquez Learning to Live Again Series

Dannie Marsden

Affinity
eBook Press
NZ
2014

Desert Blooms
© Dannie Marsden 2014

Affinity E-Book Press NZ LTD.
Canterbury, New Zealand

1st Edition

ISBN: 978-1-927282-83-0

Editor: Ruth Stanley
Cover Design: Irish Dragon Designs

Acknowledgements

I'd like to thank all the ladies at Affinity eBook Press for all their hard work and dedication. It means a lot to have someone willing to invest time into putting out enjoyable lesbian books. I'd especially like to thank Mel for all her hard work, as well as Nancy for the cover creation and Ruth for guiding me with her editing. And of course all the readers, who make what I do a pleasure.

Dedication

It takes a very special person to live and deal with a writer; our friends and families usually end up hearing about story lines and plot changes and people who aren't real…at least not to them. So I'd like to thank you and dedicate this to all of you. Your support and faith is what carries us through when we spend hours looking at a blank page. Heidi, your encouragement is never-ending; thank you for that. Know that my heart belongs only to you.

Table of Contents

Prologue

Jessica Sullivan, Special Agent with the ATF, drove the long, hot stretch of highway back to the city she had left years ago, her mind going over the past and the present and struggling with her inner demons. Sure she had been back plenty of times, but it was always a fly in and back out kind of situation, and if her visit required a stay over there was always her brother's place. She never felt the need to look up old friends or spend any longer than a few hours with people she knew from back then. This trip, she knew, was going to be entirely different. This time she was in town to find a dirty agent; she was there for however long it took her. That was the directive from above and all her arguing to send someone else—ignored.

So here she was driving her red Honda Civic Si Coupe eighty-five miles an hour down I-40, praying on one hand that she wouldn't have to deal with Lucinda Velazquez and hoping on the other that she would. She wanted to see her friend. Talking on the phone and brief conversations during the few hours they did spend together helped heal some of the wounds, but it didn't help heal them all. They had gone through the 'yes, I fucked up,' and the 'okay, I can forgive you this,' and gotten to the best friend stage again. Then they had gone through it all again; this time with Jessica being the one who had to say 'I fucked up.' With the distance between herself and her destination growing shorter by the hour, the turmoil in her stomach grew as well. The two had briefly spoken at the funeral of Luce's dad, and by that time Yvette was long gone. The Luce she spoke to then was withdrawn and unemotional, almost cold. Jessica wondered if Luce would be around this time, or if she was off on some case. "Jesus, be fair, Jessica," she said aloud as she ran her hand through her long black hair, "she is an agent; she goes where and when they tell her, just like you do." With a touch of irritation, Jessica stabbed the scan button of the radio looking for some decent music. The station stopped and in a heartbeat, Jessica was taken back in time by the song that played. The words to "I'll Stand by You" sung by The Pretenders, spoke of support and loyalty, of understanding and it hit on the one thing Jessica tried to ignore for years…she still loved Luce.

It instantly put her back in that coffee shop where they'd had coffee or tea so many times throughout the process that takes two people from friends to that special place where something more comes to life. There are moments in life that freeze in your memory; when every detail is as vivid now as when the moment first occurred. This song brought it all back for Jessica. She could recall perfectly the time of year, time of day, exactly where they sat and what they had been drinking when Luce quietly began singing along with the radio. Luce's voice was deep and rich, and had captivated Jessica, making her feel as if Luce was singing to her, as if the words of the song were meant for her and her alone. It was as if Luce had cast a spell on her. She remembered knowing in that very moment that she was head over heels in love with her. Later, after they left the coffee shop, Jessica told Luce how much she really loved her voice and was thrilled when Luce's reply was a quietly spoken, *"I love everything about you…"*

"God! If this is any indication of where my mind is gonna go during this drive, this is gonna be a long assignment," Jessica said as she reached to the center console and grabbed the bottle of water that sat in the cup holder.

It's been fifteen years, we've both moved on. It's time I got over her. It's never gonna be again and I need to accept that.

Eventually Jessica was able to pull her thoughts away from the memories and think a little about the reason she was headed to Phoenix. Allegations of dirty agents in both the DEA and ATF field offices resulted in her being given the task of finding the persons or person. She was going to be working with Douglas Tyler, who would be looking into the DEA part of the investigation, while she handled the ATF. The whole thing meant getting to know someone in a very short period of time and trusting him. Not something she was fond of doing, especially given the circumstances. She would have to chat with Joe Alverez, maybe get his thoughts since he worked for the ATF, and, of course, Luce. They may have some ideas and she trusted them both with her life. With a plan in place she activated her Bluetooth and spoke, "Call Renee, home office," and was immediately connected with her office.

"Renee Santos, how may I assist you?" she heard after the second ring.

"Renee, I need to find Joe Alverez and Lucinda Velazquez, both are in the Phoenix area. See if you can arrange for dinner with them please."

"I'm on it. How's the trip going so far, you enjoying the wind in your hair yet?" Renee replied with a teasing tone. Renee was at her desk when Jessica learned she was being sent to Phoenix. She'd heard the raised voices so she knew Jessica was not happy about this assignment.

"Oh yeah, the A/C is blasting cool air and…okay, honestly, once I got out on the road, it is relaxing and the countryside is beautiful."

"That's my girl!" Renee laughed. "I'll let you know what I can get set up for you."

"Thanks, I'll be in touch," Jessica replied and hung up. Her mind went back to the two people she loved most in Phoenix. How long had it been since they had all had time to just hang out, she wondered. It had to have been before she left town, five or six years ago. She was still with Gloria; Luce was, of course, single, and Joe was married and expecting his first child. The memory of that night was bittersweet; it was the last time they had all been together. Time and life changed things, it always stepped in and before you knew it, things happened. Within a year she and Gloria broke up and she had taken the job she had now. Actually, first, she took the job that Gloria made clear she wasn't happy about and then they broke up. Joe and Luce quit the police force and were accepted into the DEA and ATF. Luce found Yvette, broke up with her, lost her father and for a little while, herself. "Shit, I should have come to see her when all that shit was happening. Why didn't I?" Jessica questioned herself. "And say what, let me make it better and jump in the sack with you?" Shaking her head she said, "No, that wouldn't have happened…" Right… Yup, this trip is gonna be a long one.

Chapter One

Sitting on a chair in the corner of the room, Jessica flipped through the pages of a magazine, her eyes occasionally glancing over to check on the figure stretched out on the bed. Her mind replaying the voice mail she had received from Luce, "Hey, Jess, I'm on my way to Saint Luke's Park to talk to Beth. Meet me there, I want you two to meet…I know you'll love her as much as I do. Okay, see you soon." It had been three days since Luce had been shot and rushed into surgery, and the time between her eyes being open versus being closed was becoming longer; however, she still tired easily. While she slept she would drift between peaceful sleep and nightmares. Three weeks ago, their friend and fellow undercover agent Joe was killed. Jessica could only imagine Luce was dreaming of Joe's death, that she was hearing Donavon Vargas order Joe's execution and was witnessing it all over again in her nightmares. During the time Luce was awake, she would ask about Beth, her lover and Donavon's girlfriend, and it was getting harder to cover the fact that Beth wasn't there. Jessica knew she was eventually going to have to spill the beans and tell Luce what was going on, and she dreaded it. As her eyes dropped back to the pages of her *People* magazine, her mind went through questioning sessions with Beth Ryan, and the more she thought about them, the more she was positive the woman knew more than she was telling.

"Can I get some water please," Jessica heard Luce ask.

"Of course, how are you feeling?" Jess said. *She sounds stronger, that's good; means I won't be able to stall much longer, though.* She poured a small cup of water and then held the tip of the straw to Luce's dry lips.

After taking a sip, Luce was able to speak better and replied, "I feel like shit. My chest hurts and what the hell is with all these damn tubes and shit?"

"Do you want me to get the nurse?" Jessica asked with concern, worried that it may be something more than the pain from the surgery.

"I don't know…maybe…where's Beth?"

"Um, well, she was here while you were sleeping and left a bit ago. Wanted me to tell you she will be back later. So do you need anything? Want to try to sit up maybe?"

"No, I hurt," Luce replied as Jessica arranged the blankets on the bed.

When Jessica looked to Luce's face she saw the woman watching her with a slight smile. "What?" she asked as she gave a small bashful smile of her own.

"Just…just wondering when you became so, I don't know, domesticated," Luce said with a laugh before she uttered, "Crap, that hurts."

"Domesticated, huh. I've always been; you just never took the time to notice, sweetheart." Jessica spoke with love in her voice.

As her eyes closed, Luce gave a short sigh. "Yeah, I suppose I didn't, I'm sorry for that. So when did you say Beth would be back?" she asked. Luce slowly started to drift off again.

Noticing that Luce was already asleep, Jessica quietly walked to the window and looked out, her arms crossed in front of her as she struggled with her dilemma. With the sun setting on the horizon, Jessica couldn't help but feel her spirit sinking as well.

†

Beth paced the floor of the safe house as she waited for Jessica to show up. The last three days had been a nightmare. First, she heard Luce, her bodyguard, confess that she was an undercover DEA agent, then she watched Luce get shot and shoot Donavon, followed by Jessica, an ATF agent, pushing her out of the way and calling Luce "baby" and whatnot, then to the hospital where Luce was rushed to surgery. She discovered that Luce had that woman—Jessica—listed as family, and then she found herself taken into custody by federal agents. Not once in all of that had she been allowed to see Luce alone. ATF, DEA, and FBI had questioned her extensively and she couldn't even tell who else, but it was becoming more and more apparent that she was in some shit.

"I'm going to have to figure this out," she said to herself, rubbing her arms as though she were trying to warm up. Her head snapped to the door as it opened and Jessica walked in.

"What's going on with Luce? When can I go see her?" She fired questions at Jessica as soon as the door closed.

"Can you relax, you're like a broken record: 'When can I see Luce…' Jessica mimicked. "Maybe after you go through Vargas's organization again and tell us everything you know…everything."

"Look, I want to see her, and I'm pretty sure there is some law or something about you not being able to keep me here," Beth said as she advanced into the woman's personal space, hatred filling her.

"Ah, small problem there, you see I'm not the one keeping you here. If it were up to me you'd have been cut loose already, but seems the higher-ups are of the opinion that you have important information about Vargas's operation and are therefore in danger. So it looks like you'll be heading out with a marshal under the witness protection program, and unless you want to be charged with assaulting a federal agent I suggest you back off." Jessica sat down on a used sofa and propped her feet up on the coffee table that sat in front of it.

"I don't know what you're talking about. I have no clue about Donavon's business dealings. You know Luce wouldn't appreciate your treatment of me. I can't wait to see her and tell her about it."

Jessica let out a deep laugh. "Oh really? And whom do you think she is more likely to believe, you or me? Beth, you may have her ear right now, but she knows and trusts me with her life, I don't think you're there yet."

Realizing she wasn't getting anywhere with this tactic, the blond woman decided to try something else. She walked to the sofa and sat next to Jessica. Dropping her head in her hands she began to cry. Through her sobs, she said, "I'm sorry, Jessica, I just…I don't know what to do. I love Luce and not seeing her or knowing her condition is making me crazy. Please, I swear I don't know anything."

Clearing her throat, Jessica stood up, walked to the window, and looked out at the darkness. *What am I doing? Luce is going to be so pissed at me when she hears what I'm doing.* "Well, Beth, here's the thing, I'm not sure I believe you and, honestly, I know the DEA and FBI don't."

Getting up and walking to Jessica, Beth changed her tactic once again. Reaching up with her hands she gently began rubbing the other woman's shoulders. "I don't mean to be so emotional. It's just that a lot has happened and I'm having trouble processing it all. Wow, from the feel of it so are you; your shoulders are so tense. Why don't you sit down and let me give you a massage? I'm pretty good at helping to release tension."

"What they hell are you doing?" Jessica said as she turned and frowned. "I'll deal with my own tension, thank you…gotta wonder what Luce would say about your offer."

"Please, you knew Luce a long time ago. As you said, I have her ear now and I'm pretty sure she would never believe I came on to you."

†

Moving restlessly in her sleep, Luce drifted between visions of a gun trained on Joe's head, Joe pleading with his eyes for her to do something, her digging a hole and rolling Joe's body into that hole. Her dreams shifted to her running as she pulled Beth with her, trying to get away from Donavon Vargas. She heard bullets zipping past her, felt her lungs burning as they struggled for oxygen and the rush of adrenaline as fear coursed through her body. Her drug-hazed brain recalled the fear of knowing that Vargas knew who she was, of knowing he wanted her dead. She had been the other undercover agent who worked to bring down his organization, the only one that had direct knowledge of his actions and was still breathing. Well, okay, there was also the fact that she had been sleeping with his woman, but at this point who the hell was gonna be that picky? The simple fact was he'd escaped custody, had found her and was now shooting at her.

In her nightmares, she saw herself dragging Beth to the wooded area as bullets zinged past them, she remembered crouching behind a tree and the beads of sweat on her brow as she heard the twigs crack behind her and she came face-to-face with Vargas. She felt the bullet hit her chest, and everything went black. Everything but the faint voice, the one that sounded so much like Jessica's telling her to stay with her… Luce's eyes flew open, her chest burned and she could see the setting sun from the window.

Chapter Two

"Hey, Red, call for you on line two." With an inward groan Amanda reached for the phone on her desk. *At this rate, I'm never gonna get this damned piece ready for publishing,* she thought even as she picked up the phone.

"Amanda Murphy speaking," she spoke as she leaned back in her chair.

"If you want a good story, look into Donavon Vargas, Beth Ryan, and the death of Judge Marcus Stone." Then the line went dead. With a frown, she looked at the receiver in her hand before she replaced it. *What the hell was that about?*

"Ron, did you get a name of that last caller?" Her voice was louder than normal as she stood up and walked toward him.

"No, why?" Ron Adams looked up over his shoulder at her as her hand softly touched him.

The look on her face got his attention. "What's up, Amanda?" he asked as he turned to face the woman. Moving a chair next to the desk Amanda sat down and crossed her left leg over her right knee, "Just a really weird call. Did they ask for me specifically?"

"Yeah,"

"Didn't give a name, just asked for me?"

"Yeah, Marcy is probably swamped in reception and accidently hit my line instead of yours. When I picked up and identified myself, the person asked for you." Ron asked as his interest piqued.

"The caller said if I wanted a good story that I should check out the connection between Donavan Vargas, Beth Ryan, and Marcus Stone. Why does that name sound familiar?"

"Seriously you don't remember? The ATF shot Donavon Vargas to death a few days ago after he escaped police custody while being transported to court. Not much is being said on the whole thing. And Marcus Stone was the federal judge who was killed when he walked into a ongoing robbery in his home."

"That's right, Donavon escaped along with…oh what were their names…Drew Jones and Paul Dunham, right? Both were suspected of arms trafficking to Mexico. Wasn't there talk of it being military-grade firepower?" the red-haired woman asked as she sat forward, sensing a story indeed.

"Yeah, but what's that got to do with Judge Stone?" Ron asked as he sat back in his seat, the pencil in his hand twirling through his fingers.

"I have no idea. At this point I have so much on my plate I'm not even sure I want to find out," Amanda said. "What about you, how's your piece on lost hope and humanity going?" she teased and laughed at the running joke between them. Both Ron and Amanda worked as investigative journalists for a local Phoenix newspaper. Ron was working on a series about the use of steroids in local high schools. While it was nothing earth shattering, it was proving to be an interesting series as far as Amanda was concerned. Amanda worked in a deeper, darker, realm; one where if she stumbled on something big it could earn her death threats or an award. She didn't worry much on what danger she stepped in; it wasn't that she had a death wish, she just couldn't walk away from something that grabbed her interest. Most of the time that meant corruption in government, at the local level or higher. Something inside her screamed that she shouldn't let this tip go. A federal judge linked to a dead drug and arms dealer and his girlfriend? Oh yes, that was interesting indeed. She would have to do some digging after all, no matter how much she had on her plate.

"Hey, wanna grab a sandwich or something, I'm starved," she spoke as she stood up.

"Sure, I can tell you about my column coming out this week!" Ron said with a smile as he stood up and reached for his jacket. The two walked toward the door, chatting about their columns and teasing one another as they left.

Close to three hours later, Amanda was walking into the offices of the ATF and DEA, hoping to find someone that knew about Vargas and his death.

"Excuse me, I'm Amanda Murphy, a reporter with the *Phoenix Sun*, and I was looking for some information about the death of Donavon Vargas. I understand he was arrested a few days prior to his shooting. Is that true?"

"I'm sorry, I can't help you. Why don't you talk to SAC Tyler…follow me and I'll take you to his office," the lean man spoke.

"Thank you, Agent…?"

"Vance, Agent Jason Vance at your service," the man said with a wide smile as he bowed slightly.

With a smile of her own, Amanda replied, "Very nice to meet you, Agent Vance. So how long have you been an agent?"

"Oh, I am a rookie agent; I just started about six months ago. Here we are." Agent Vance knocked on the door. "Special Agent in Charge Tyler, this is Amanda Murphy, a reporter for the *Sun*. She would like to talk to you about the Vargas case." Getting up from his chair Tyler walked around the desk and toward the door, extending his hand as he approached the tall redhead. "Thank you, Vance. It's pleasure to meet you, Ms. Murphy; I'm a huge fan of your work. Please come in and have a seat." He moved back to allow

Amanda in and motioned to a chair in front of his desk. "I'm not sure how I can help you."

"Well, here's where I'm at. I'm doing some research on Donavon Vargas, and I know he was arrested for dealing arms not too long ago. Is there anything you can tell me about that? "Ms. Murphy, I really can't comment on anything since the case against the other men is still open."

"I see. I did some reading before I came over and I'm wondering what you can tell me about Mr. Vargas's shooting. He escaped from police custody on the way to his court hearing and was shot to death in a park, and, yet, no one is talking about it. Interesting don't you think?"

"You're a reporter, I would imagine that you find or look for coincidences in just about anything." Tyler sat back in his chair and studied the reporter. His face never betrayed the thoughts racing through his head. *Shit, this one isn't going to let this go. And it's gonna cause a real shit storm if she spills anything she finds out.*

"What about the second individual reportedly shot in the park that day? Come on, SAC Tyler, give me a break. Investigative reporter or not, there's something here and we both know it. If not me, then someone else will get to the bottom of things and not everyone has the integrity to keep the innocent out of the line of fire."

"Ms. Murphy, even if I wanted to, I really can't tell you anything that would help you. Yes Vargas, Dunham, and Jones were recently arrested on arms charges. They were all released due to some mix-up in the evidence locker. Vargas was picked up again on a different charge, with plenty of evidence. On the way to his hearing, members of his organization helped him escape. Officers later responded to a shootout at a park to find Vargas dead and a DEA agent fighting for her life."

"How did the agent know he would be at the park?" Amanda asked.

"I don't believe she did," Tyler replied.

"So it was just a coincidence that a federal agent and the head of a drug and arms organization happened to be at the same park? Come on, Agent Tyler, I'm not that stupid and neither is anyone else."

"I can't tell you any more than I already have. In fact, I may have told you more than I should have." Tyler stood up and walked toward the redhead with his hand held out as an invitation to stand. "So how about you let me get back to my job. There are a lot of bad guys out there."

With a soft sigh Amanda uncrossed her legs and elegantly rose out of the seat. With a smile, she extended her hand in a gesture of friendship and said, "Thank you for your time, SAC Tyler. If it's all the same to you, I'm going to keep digging and see what I can come up with."

Straightening to his full height, he said, "Ms. Murphy, I can't stress how much I would discourage that; however, I know from your record that you won't pay attention, so I ask that you at least be discreet in your questions and watch your six." Tyler put his own hand out to shake the reporter's hand.

"I'll take it under advisement," Amanda said with a smile and a twinkle in her eye and walked out of the man's office.

†

Knowing she had rattled Tyler during her visit, Amanda waited in her car to see if he would come out of the office building. She was not disappointed. She watched as Tyler walked out of the building, got in his car, and drove quickly out of the parking lot. Through her years as an investigative journalist, Amanda had learned how to follow someone and not be seen, and that's what she did now. Tyler's distracted way of driving, not checking his mirrors, drifting into the other lane every now and then, made it easy for her to follow him. "Where are you going, Agent?" she murmured as she maneuvered the traffic and turns while keeping the man in sight. Realizing that he was traveling in the direction of the hospital, Amanda took a chance and pulled ahead and waited for him to arrive.

"Well, well, Agent Tyler, who are you visiting?" Amanda asked herself as she followed Tyler, making sure she kept the man in sight as they walked through the hospital hallways. Once she was able to see the room number, she walked to a waiting room and waited for him to leave. Tyler didn't stay long and soon she was walking toward the room he had just left. The door opened again and an attractive, dark, slender woman walked out past her. With a nod and a smile, Amanda kept on walking until she reached a hallway that she could turn into. Carefully peeking around the corner, Amanda looked to make sure the coast was clear before she made her way back toward the room.

Carefully opening the door, the redhead peeked in and saw a raven-haired woman sleeping. Being as quiet as she could, Amanda made her way into the room and to the side of the bed. *Well, who are you dark and gorgeous?* she thought as she looked at the woman. Amanda glanced at the wall and saw a whiteboard where found the patient's name. She then looked back at the woman and noticed a chart on the bedside table, "Well, Amanda, it looks like it's your lucky day," she said quietly to herself as she walked toward the table. She read the name on the chart. It matched the one on the whiteboard so she filed it in her brain and continued reading. As she read Luce turned her head and mumbled incoherently, causing Amanda to pause. *No, no...stay asleep just a moment longer,* she prayed. She froze waiting to make sure the patient wasn't going to open her eyes and see her. When she was sure the woman was still asleep, she placed the chart back where she'd found it and silently backed toward the door, then slid out into the hallway. With a sigh of relief she walked toward the elevator but froze when she spotted Agent Tyler and the same attractive woman she saw coming out of the hospital room speaking to a doctor. She quickly turned on her heel and went in search of another elevator and out the front doors of the hospital.

†

Back at her desk Amanda quickly fired up her computer and did a search on the name she memorized from the medical chart: Lucinda Velazquez.

"Let's see what you're all about Lucinda Velazquez," she said as she opened the first item that popped up in search. It was an article about some medal she had received as well as her acceptance into the DEA. Glancing through the rest of the article, Amanda closed it then pulled up the next item. This one told of an accident she was involved in on the night of her promotion, resulting in the death of a child. "Oh, shit," Amanda said as she continued reading. The article stated, from witness accounts of the accident, the vehicle Velazquez and her girlfriend were in had been hit from behind and sent spinning into oncoming traffic. Velazquez suffered broken ribs, and a concussion and the girlfriend had a mild concussion. Amanda went on to read that even with her injuries, Velazquez still tried to pry open the door of the other car to save the child. From what Amanda read, the woman was a hero. "Okay, so Ms. Hero, how'd you end up with a gunshot wound in the hospital?" she asked as she sat back in her seat.

Chapter Three

ATF Agent Mason Cafferty paced the room pissed as hell. "What the fuck do you mean the operation is on hold for the time being? Just because Vargas is dead doesn't mean that we can't continue with things."

"Yes, that is exactly what I'm saying," a deep voice replied calmly.

"Bullshit! Who left you in charge of things…look we can still all get rich. I still have informants; I still have contacts, just like you do."

"I'm well aware of that, but I'm telling you we lay low for now. We have time, so relax."

"Fuck that, I'm meeting with some of our contacts, get things rolling again. I know that some of the dealers are running low; I also know that groups down south are itching for those guns."

"What part of 'we are laying low for now' do you not fucking understand?" the deep voice shouted. "There is too much at risk right now, and I don't give a shit how many contacts you fucking have. I won't sacrifice my people because you're on some fucking power trip. Now get your ass out of my sight and get back to finding who the fuck that second fed was, because until you do *nothing* moves."

"You stupid fuck! We're wasting a shitload of time and losing just as much money," Cafferty shouted, slamming his hands on the desk that separated him and the new 'boss.' Within a split second, he was staring down the barrel of an FN Herstal Five-seven and had no doubt the prick holding it would fire if he pushed further. As the man stood up, still holding the pistol to the agent's face, he spoke with a cold, low voice, "Do we understand each other, Agent Cafferty? You won't do a goddamn thing without checking with me first."

"Yeah, I got it," Cafferty responded as he forced his anger and resentment down. Backing up, he continued, "How about I get my 'ass' back to the office and see what I can come up with."

"You do that," the tall, dark-haired man said as he put the pistol back in the holster clipped to his belt beneath his expensive suit jacket. He sat back down in the leather chair behind the oak desk.

Mason stormed out of the building and down the alley to his car. Once inside he pulled the door shut and slammed the palms of his hands into the steering wheel as a string of obscenities flew from his mouth. "Fucking Vargas, you sure as hell did a fucking good job of keeping all the players from knowing each other didn't you, ya bastard," he shouted as his frustration grew. Just who was that fucker to think he deserved to take over the business? Did he put in as much sweat and risk as he had? "FUCK!" he roared as he pulled out his cell phone and punched in a number. "Enjoy where you're sitting for now, you won't be there long, I promise," he said as he waited for the man on the other end of the call to pick up.

"Foreman, listen, I want you to find out everything you can about Vargas's operatives and I mean all of them, anyone he so much as looked at for any length of time. Focus on anyone with the nickname 'the Chameleon.' Yes, I know I have a shitload of info, but I want more. Look, I just walked out of a meeting with the new boss, and no one knows who the hell he is. … How the hell do I know? He said he was very close to Vargas and was going to take over the business. … Yeah, well, the only person I can think of that potentially has that power is the Chameleon. I'll see you in a bit." With his lips pursed tightly he started his car and drove away.

☨

Thomas Sullivan put the key to his apartment into the lock and turned it. Opening the door, the only two things he looked forward to at the moment were seeing his sister Jessica and a nice hot shower. The flight into town had been long, and the meeting he had just left half an hour ago, stressful. "Hey, sis, you here?" he shouted, not really expecting an answer. *I should have given her a heads-up that I was coming in today.* He thought as he went to his room and put his suitcase down on the floor. He tossed his jacket on the bed and rolled his shoulders to ease the knots. Walking toward the bathroom he passed his sister's room and noticed the unmade bed with rumpled sheet and clothes scattered around. "Looks like you had some big fun, sis. Way to go!" he said aloud with a smile.

Tom closed the bathroom door behind him, turned on the water and adjusted the temperature as the spray shot from the showerhead. He stripped as the water heated up, then stepped under the spray with a groan. The hot water splashed down over his dark hair and shoulders, slowly easing the tension that rested at the base of his neck. Taking a few moments to simply enjoy, he closed his eyes and rolled his head letting the moist heat do its job. Relaxing for the first time in hours, Tom turned, closed his eyes and lifted his face toward the spray. As the water streamed down his broad chest, he sighed, wondering when Jess would get in. Maybe he would call her and let her know he was back. He couldn't wait to have some time to relax and just hang with his big sis. Geez, he thought, how long had it been since they'd seen each other? Nearly five years.

As he wiped dripping water out of his eyes, he reached for the shampoo and grinned. He'd matured some since then, sort of. Filled out too, he thought, as he flexed a muscled arm just because. She'd still be beautiful as ever, that much was a given. Probably still as serious, but hey, no one was perfect. It didn't matter he thought, as he quickly dumped shampoo into the palm of his hand and started massaging it into his scalp, she'd be just as eager to see him as he was her. Quickly sticking his head back underneath the spray, he scrubbed his hands vigorously over his head until the water ran clear. Reaching for the soap he grinned as he covered himself in lather, he was still excited to see her. She was definitely the distraction he needed for a while and he was going to enjoy every minute of it while he could. He decided he'd call her as soon as he was done to let her know he was there and looking forward to an evening of catching up. Of course, he thought as he rinsed off, she might have other plans. Maybe even with whatever hot little number had helped her muss the bed. With a little grin and a shake of his head, he decided not to go there. Thomas took the time to shave, then dragged on a pair of ratty, dark blue sweats and an old AC/DC T-shirt that had seen better days. Feeling totally relaxed, he flipped open his cell as he strode down the hall toward the kitchen and punched in Jess's number. He smiled when the call went right to voice mail.

"Hey sis! I'm home and you're not! Get your ass over here so we can suck down some suds and lie to each other about whatever comes to mind." He flipped the phone closed as he yanked open the fridge door and perused the contents, happy to see there was indeed beer inside. With a grin he thought, of course there would be beer, Jess liked beer too and if memory served she had always made sure there was some in stock. "So what else do you have in here to eat, sis? I'm kind of hungry, please have some bologna or salami." As Tom rummaged through the fridge he found a couple of cartons of leftover Chinese, some leftover lasagna, an assortment of cheeses and finally a package of both bologna and salami, along with lettuce in the crisper, mustard and mayo in the door. "Yes…you rock, big sis!"

With an armful of items and a beer in his hand, he walked to the counter where he set everything down and opened the loaf of multigrain bread, taking out two slices. He reached out and punched the power button of the iPod station and immediately the gravelly voice of Chad Kruger and his band filled the room. With his head bobbing to the beat he slathered the bread with mayo, added lettuce, salami, some cheese then mustard and the second slice of bread. Grabbing the bottle of beer, he twisted the cap off, took a long swallow and pitched the cap into the trash. Then he grabbed the sandwich with his other hand and walked to the window of the living room. As he took a bite he couldn't help but think how good it felt to be home.

✝

As Jessica walked out of the hospital to her car she pulled her cell phone out of her purse and found several missed calls, one of them being from her brother, Tom. With a broadening smile she listened to the message and headed home, eager to put an end to the day. Tomorrow she would have to deal with telling Luce that Beth was now in witness protection and she wouldn't be seeing her again; not something she was looking forward to. Driving home, Jessica tried to not think of the million questions Luce would be asking, nor the answers she would or wouldn't have, but it was an impossible feat. "Oh, just stop thinking, for Christ sake," she muttered as she punched the radio on and began to drum her fingers to the song playing. In a short while, she was pulling up to the house.

"Tom, where are you?" Jessica shouted, dropping her briefcase as soon as she was in the door of the apartment.

"In here, sis." She heard the voice answer from the kitchen and headed that way. As she hit the entrance she saw her brother coming toward her with his arms open. She walked into them with a grateful sigh and let the tears fall.

"Hey, what's this…why the tears?" The tall man asked as his arms closed tight around the woman he hadn't seen in five years. Feeling his sister shaking in his arm bothered him. "Come on, let's go into the living room, get yourself together and tell me what's wrong. You're making me feel all protective and shit," he said softly, trying to get his sister to calm down.

"Oh hell, I didn't mean to fall apart of like this," Jessica said as she pulled back and wiped her eyes and sniffled. Clearing her throat she continued, "God, it's good to see you!"

"Same here, sis. So, come on, tell me what the tears were all about," Tom said as they sat down in the living room. Tom's deep blue eyes studied his sister and saw something different in her. A maturity he'd never noticed before maybe, but there was something else, something he couldn't put his finger on. She'd always been a knockout, but hell she was his sister, of course he would say she was beautiful. For whatever reason, today he truly looked at her as a woman and saw all of her beauty. The fact that someone had caused tears to fall from her eyes pissed him off and he wanted to know why, and who…especially the who part of that equation.

"Really, it's not a big deal, I think I was just so happy to see you again, and it's been a long couple of weeks. Do you remember Luce Velazquez?" She asked as she sat back and got herself under control again.

"How can I not. Goddamn we all had a blast that summer of my freshman year of college," Tom replied. His smile grew brighter at the memory of those years. "How is she doing? Damn, I haven't thought of her in years; you two were good together…what the heck happened between you guys?"

"Things…anyway, a couple of days after I got into town she was shot, a few more inches and the bullet would have pierced her heart…we would have lost her."

"Oh, my god, is she all right? Did they find out who did it?" Tom asked, sitting forward in his seat, his elbows on his knees and fingers clasped tightly.

"Yes, they did. Anyway, I suppose that is part of the reason for the meltdown. I haven't had a chance to take a breath, and, well, seeing you just…I have someone to lean on and lose it in front of I guess." Jessica laughed. "So tell me, what exotic place did you just come in from; and yes, I'm changing the subject, I don't want to talk about work let alone think about it."

"Do you wanna go see her? I mean, I'd totally understand if you did."

"No. I had just left the hospital before I got your message and came straight home. I'll stop in and see her on my way to work tomorrow. Hey, what do you think about going with me?"

"Oh, I would but already made plans with a friend in town; maybe we can see her tomorrow night?"

"Yeah, that sounds like a plan," Jessica replied as she sat forward. "So have you eaten anything other than a sandwich?"

"Well, no not really." Tom laughed.

"Okay, I'm not sure what all I have in the fridge, but want to come talk with me while I look; maybe I'll find something to whip up for dinner. What do you say?"

"Sounds good, and if you have anything I'll even help. How about that? Tom teased.

Brother and sister made their way to the kitchen teasing each other as they went.

Jessica walked to the fridge band opened the door. As she glanced over the shelves, she realized there really wasn't anything other than beer, and the items that Tom took out earlier to make his sandwich. She opened the freezer and found she had nothing in there either.

"Well, good news is you don't have to do anything. Bad news is, I don't have anything that resembles a decent meal. So, you got any ideas?" she asked as she closed the freezer door and turned to look at her brother.

"Why doesn't that surprise me?" Tom laughed.

"Yeah, well, I've been a bit busy," Jessica replied with a smile on her face.

"All right, so we can do takeout, or we can go out. What do you feel like doing?" Tom asked as he leaned against the counter.

"Giovanni's?" Jessica asked.

Tom's smile grew big at the mention of the small family-owned restaurant. Both Tom and Jessica had fond memories from childhood and their times in college of the Italian restaurant.

"You said the magic word. God, I haven't had good Italian food like they serve in years," Tom replied.

"Really? With all the globe-trotting you do? I'd have thought you'd have stopped at all the quaint little places Italy."

"Nothing ever came close to the food at Giovanni's. I think it's because of the memories there. Angelina was hot," Tom said with a laugh as he thought of the youngest daughter who had a very wild side.

Chapter Four

The next morning Luce woke to once again find Jessica sitting in the chair, this time reading through a file. As Luce looked at her, she couldn't help but compare the woman she saw today and the woman she had known years ago. This one was more mature and sure of herself, she carried herself with confidence. But there was something else, though Luce couldn't put her finger on it. Maybe it was the beauty in her face that hadn't been there before. "Where is Beth? She cleared her throat, looking around the room, wondering why Beth hadn't been by.

"Well, good morning to you too. How are you feeling?" Jessica put the file in her briefcase and uncrossed her legs.

"Like I have tubes sticking out of my body and was hit by a Mack truck. How do you think I feel? Where's Beth?"

"My, aren't we a ray of sunshine." Jessica let out a sigh before she continued, "Look, about Beth…I hate to have to tell you this but Beth was taken into witness protection early this morning. I have no idea where she is."

"What do you mean in witness protection, why?" Luce struggled to sit up.

"Hey, whoa there, you need to be careful." She quickly stood and reached for Luce.

Breathing hard, Luce laid back, groaning between breaths. "You better talk, right now."

"You need to take it easy," Jessica said with authority in her voice as she watched the dark-haired woman closely.

"Okay, I will, just tell me what's going on."

"All the agencies agree that Beth knows more about Vargas's organization than she is saying, and unfortunately the only way to keep her safe at the moment is to hide her away somewhere."

"Are you kidding me? Beth doesn't know anything."

"You have to see it from their point of view. She was with him for quite a while, and there is always pillow talk."

"Doesn't matter. She spent her time shopping and spending his money. He wasn't the type to engage in pillow talk," Luce spoke as she closed her eyes.

"You weren't with them when they were alone. You don't know what went on between them. Honestly, there is every possibility that she knows something that will help us nail every one of them."

"She doesn't. Don't you think I'd know if she did?"

"I think you were more focused on screwing her than paying attention to what was happening," Jessica said in frustration.

"How dare you imply I wasn't doing my job," Luce shot back.

"Joe is dead. You were sleeping with Vargas's lady. How much attention did you really pay to things going on?" Jessica fired back, her frustration growing.

"Don't…I am not responsible for Joe's death. There was nothing I could have done to stop it, not without getting killed myself," Luce said in a defeated tone. A tear rolled down her cheek and she grimaced in pain.

"Babe, I wasn't there; I don't believe you were responsible for Joe's death but the fact is you were involved with Vargas's woman. I don't think you were totally focused on things. And sorry to say, but I think you're blinded by your feelings and not being objective about Beth."

"How could you let her leave without letting me see her, you could have done something…" Luce said quietly.

"There was nothing I could have done," Jessica replied. "I'm sorry."

"Find her, let me at least talk to her, please," Luce said as she looked straight into Jessica's eyes.

"Luce, I can't, you know that. Vargas's organization is looking for her, at least that's what our sources are saying. That means she is in danger. She is safe wherever she is and you know that."

"I KNOW that I need to see her…to talk to her. Damn it, Jess, I love her."

Turning away from Luce, Jessica rolled her eyes and walked to the window. As she looked out she said, "All the more reason to leave it alone. When it's safe for her come back she will. Look, I need to get back work. I'll be back to see you after lunch." She turned back and looked at Luce. Luce looked lost. Was she really doing the right thing, she wondered. Jessica walked to the bedside and reached out to touch Luce's arm. "Can I bring you anything?" she asked.

"Just a number that I can call Beth at," Luce replied as she closed her eyes.

Jessica sighed and walked toward the door, both knowing she couldn't fulfill that request.

✝

At the office, Jessica's morning didn't get any better. Poring through files, the only thing she could come up with in her investigation of a dirty agent dealt with James Foreman, the agent she had placed on leave the night Joe was killed. Some cases he worked on had evidence disappear, which led to criminals walking, low-level, but criminals nonetheless. She thought back to the paunchy man and the disrespect he'd displayed toward her. Was there something more to his behavior she wondered? Tossing the file onto her desk, she sat back and pushed her fingers through her hair as she sighed.

Her stomach reminded her that it was after lunch and she had yet to eat. She rubbed the bridge of her nose and scooted her chair back. She grabbed her purse from the bottom desk drawer and walked toward her office door. As she was closing the door she spotted Mason Cafferty walking toward her, if you could call what he was doing a walk. It almost reminded her of a panther stalking its prey, or maybe a snake slithering up on an unsuspecting creature. Either way it made her stomach roll, and the last thing she wanted was to have to deal with the man.

"SAC Sullivan, can I have a minute?"

Putting a smile on her face she spoke, "Agent, what can I do for you?"

Oh I'm sure you could do a lot for me, maybe bend over that desk in your office for a start, he thought, but what he said was, in his opinion, a very charming invitation to lunch. "Well, I don't believe it's so much what you can do for me but what I could do for you. How about joining me for lunch? We can get to know each other a bit then I can fill you in on the cases Foreman and I worked together." When he saw Jessica hesitate he continued, "Come on, I'll buy and it won't even go on the expense account. I know a great little Italian place that serves a fantastic cacciatore, and an out-of-this-world tiramisu, what do you say?" Jessica was about to say no, but she was hungry and she needed to get out of the office building, so she responded, "Sure, why not. But I would prefer you put it on the expense account."

"Why, I would consider it an honor to pay, and you could look at it as an olive branch so to speak."

"I would rather you not feel I owe you anything, so it's expense account, I pay for my own meal or I don't go."

"Okay, okay, expense account it is. Ladies first," he said as he stepped aside to let Jessica in front of him. Once outside he walked next to her, guiding her to where he was parked. When they walked up to his car, a sleek pearl-gray 2013

Lexus LFA, he could see that she was impressed. Flashy for sure and not something most would have thought an agent of the DEA or ATF would drive. As he opened the door for her, he told her the car could go from zero to sixty in 3.6 seconds. He realized she didn't care when he looked at her face. Cafferty walked around to his side of the car, his teeth grinding. *Stupid bitch doesn't know enough to be impressed. God knows she could never afford a car like this.* As he slid into the driver's seat he noticed Jessica looking around the interior of his car. *Ah, so you are somewhat impressed.* He continued to tell her more about the car.

"Nice car, Cafferty, had to have set you back a pretty penny," she said casually.

"Oh, yeah, that's for sure. But it suits me, don't you think?" Cafferty answered with his cocky grin firmly in place. Jessica rolled her eyes, which made Cafferty laugh. "Oh, come on, Jessie, you know it does and you know I look damn good driving it," he said as he continued to laugh.

"Yes, Agent Cafferty, it is a very nice car, and…it suits you, but please remember to call me SAC Sullivan, not Jessie. This isn't a date remember."

"Yeah, I remember. I just thought we could get comfortable with one another is all. My apologies, SAC Sullivan, it won't happen again," Cafferty spoke as he started the car and popped it into reverse. Without a second thought he threw the car into gear and sped off in the direction of the parking lot exit, ignoring the voice in his head that shouted about teaching the bitch a lesson she wouldn't soon forget.

"So tell me, Agent Cafferty, how long have you been with Phoenix field office?" Jessica asked, trying to break the uncomfortable silence that had settled inside the car.

"Been with the agency for about ten years now," Cafferty replied as his fingers drummed on the steering wheel. "What about you?"

"Little over fifteen," Jessica answered, her brain calculating the time. "Did you grow up in Phoenix?" she asked, realizing that for as much as she had read his personnel file she couldn't remember.

"There ya go, not that hard is it?" He smiled as he took his eyes off the road and looked at her.

"Excuse me?"

"Being polite, making conversation…and no I actually transferred here from Florida."

She answered his smile, with a smile of her own and let out a sigh. "No, it isn't that hard." Looking out the window she continued, "Look, I'm sorry for being such a bitch, it's just been a long few weeks…month…month and a half…god, has it been that long?"

"Yeah, it has," Cafferty replied as he returned his gaze to the traffic ahead. "You never said why you're here. I mean other than to take over the cases Foreman worked on, and honestly that doesn't make any sense."

The question hit too close for Jessica's comfort and she turned to look at him. "I just go where I'm told and do what I'm told you know. Trust me ending up back here was the last thing I wanted." *Fuck, Jessica, shut up! Don't give him more to question.* "What part of Florida did you come from?" she asked, hoping to sidetrack the man.

"Miami, actually, thought I'd get away from the drug runners there and find a bit of peace here."

"I see that worked well for you." Jessica smiled at him. "How well do you get along with Agent Foreman, what kind of guy is he?" she asked, hoping she sounded casual.

"He's a decent guy, I suppose, a hard worker. I get along with him fine," Cafferty answered as he turned into a parking lot of the restaurant. "Let's go in and find a table. We can talk more about him inside." Cafferty turned off the car, got out and met Jessica as she stepped out. Once inside and seated, they had ordered their drinks and meal then Cafferty spoke. "I know Foreman is on leave and you put him there. I just don't think you know what you're doing, SAC Sullivan."

"Tell me why you feel that way."

"Jesus, the man's record speaks for itself!" Cafferty exclaimed. "He has had busts that no one else thought about going after; he has informants that pass credible information. What more do you want?"

Jessica took a sip of her coffee as she thought about how to answer and gazed into the dark liquid. "Tell me about these informants, the cases you two worked."

"Jessica…may I call you Jessica for now? I mean, I realize around other agents it's out of line and all." When Jessica nodded he continued, "Honestly, there are too many cases to tell you all of them, but there is the Rosas case. It was a small meth operation on the east side. Members decided that their distribution area was getting too small so they started selling in schools of neighboring areas. When some people decided to oppose them they killed them."

"How many convictions on that case?" Jessica asked.

"Ten arrests, two received life for the murders, and the rest pleaded down but doing time."

"I see, what else?"

"Okay, there's the Wallace case. Large runner going through from California. Nabbed fifty kilos of white powder, five convictions on that case and two of those turned informants and gave up three smaller runners in the area."

"Nice."

"Yeah, took some scum off the street and all due to Foreman," Cafferty said proudly.

"Did you ever find evidence missing or incomplete files in any of the cases you worked with him?"

"No, I usually logged in the evidence myself," Cafferty said as he leaned forward.

"Did you follow the cases after you testified?"

"Hell, not always. You know how it goes, always another case to work. Why are you asking?"

"I'm looking through some cases that Foreman worked and there are a few cases where evidence or files have been misplaced. Tell me, Agent Cafferty, how do you think that happens?"

"Maybe that bitch, Velazquez. I think she has it in for us guys and is able to slip in and out of the evidence locker," the man answered, closely watching Jessica's reaction.

Jessica watched the man as he watched her, and asked, "Why do you think that, and what would Agent Velazquez have to gain from that?"

"Hell, I don't know, but she hates me and would do anything she can to keep me from advancing in the job. I can't figure out what she has against Foreman, though. He has said that she is gunning for him too."

"Why does she hate you? But that aside, the cases are all ones that you and Foreman worked or that he oversaw. None had anything to do with Agent Velazquez and there was no reason for her to even look through anything. So that is why he is on leave, and will remain there until the investigation is complete. I can honestly say that it is very doubtful that he will be returning."

Cafferty turned red as he said in a tight voice, "Why does it matter, she is a bitch who acts like she owns the fucking place. Are you really gonna stand by as a good man is ruined while a drunken bitch is allowed to hang around. Rumor is she is a member of the carpet-munchers club, yet she is allowed to stay and wear a badge. That's fucking disrespectful and a travesty. Tell me, are you lookin' at me too?"

"Enough, Agent Cafferty. Agent Velazquez's sexual preference isn't our concern and policy makes it illegal to even question her on it."

"Yeah, whatever. What she really needs is five minutes with me, a real man, to show her what she is missing; she needs to experience what a man can do," Cafferty stated, completely ignoring the fact that his voice was rising and drawing attention to the table.

"Agent, you are about to be brought up on sexual harassment charges, and, as far as I'm concerned, this meeting is over. Excuse me, may I have my check, please," Jessica said as the manager walked toward them. Jessica could see the manager was clearly eager to put an end to Cafferty's rant and was all too pleased to inform Jessica that the bill would be taken care of if they would just leave.

Cafferty was boiling now as he quickly pushed out of his seat, threw down his napkin and stormed out of the restaurant, leaving Jessica to speak with the man. *Bitch can find her own way back to the office.* With Cafferty storming out Jessica took the opportunity to apologize to the manager. "I'm sorry about that. It seems my colleague has forgotten his manners. I'll take care of the bill, but thank you for offering to cover it." Once finished she walked out of the restaurant and hailed a taxi for the ride back to the office. Her thoughts on the way Cafferty had spoken about a fellow agent and her friend. What is going on there? she wondered. Her thoughts went back to something Maggie, the secretary they had put at her door when she arrived, had told her happened at the meeting held the day after Joe's murder. If memory served, it was something about an argument or something like that. *Well shit, I'm gonna have to dig out of Luce what that was all about,* she thought. Pulling out her cell phone she called Douglas Tyler, Luce's boss, maybe he could shed some light on the subject. "Doug, Jessica here. Do you have some time to talk this afternoon, preferably away from the office? Great, I'll see you there," she said and then disconnected from the call. With her head pounding and the heartburn starting, she wondered if her day could get any worse.

Chapter Five

Mason Cafferty slammed the car door as he walked toward the black Lincoln, His mood was crappy and his face showed it. What he had hoped would be a nice lunch with Jessica Sullivan had turned into a 'how to do his job' speech, or at least that's how he took it. On top of that, he found himself growing hard when he talked about showing that bitch Velazquez what a man was like, and that pissed him off. How could his body betray him like that? Shit, it was as if he was back in high school getting a hard-on whenever a pretty girl smiled at him. Reaching the door of the Lincoln he pulled it open and grabbed the man behind the wheel by the collar, pulling him out. With his face inches from the man he growled, "You had better have something I want to hear or I'm through."

"Jesus, Cafferty, loosen up, you're choking me," the man said through gasping breaths.

"Do I look like I give a shit?" Cafferty said as he loosened his grip. "What have you found out, and so help me if you say nothing, I'll shoot you right where you stand."

"How many times I gotta tell you, it's hard for me to find anything out," Foreman said. When he thought he saw Cafferty reaching for his gun he rushed to say, "But, I may have found something I'm not sure yet. Word on the street is that Ryan is in protective custody. A couple of guys are saying they think she is out in Montana, I'm still waiting on confirmation though."

"I give you a week and this is the shit you bring me? I *need* a fucking address, something other than this 'some guys said' bullshit."

"Look, I'm working on it, I swear," Foreman said as he wiped the sweat from his brow. Mason couldn't help but get a small amount of satisfaction and gave a small smile when he saw the look on Foreman's face. He could see the man really thought he was dead.

"I'm tryin'. No one is saying crap about Vargas, the Ryan bitch, or anything else for that matter. Why don't we just let things settle down a bit, things will loosen up, then info will flow like shit."

"I can't afford to let things settle. Ryan has information on *all* of Vargas's contacts, his dealers, his connections…and right now head of this organization is up for grabs. Do you know who the prick dealt with? You tell me that and I'll let things settle down. Got it?"

"Yeah, I got it. There is nothing as to who the Chameleon is, and I can't find anyone alive who has worked with, or admits to having worked with or for him. It's like he's a goddamn ghost or something."

"There has to be someone who knows who this prick is, and can identify him. Why the hell can't you find him?"

Tired of being yelled at and treated as if he were stupid, Foreman shouted, "Fuck! I'll place a couple of ads in all the major papers asking anyone that knows of him to contact us! How about that? Christ, I'm doing all I can to find anything on him, but this guy is smart and doesn't make mistakes."

Ignoring that Foreman just raised his voice to him Cafferty said, "Fine, what about Velazquez? What have you found out about her? There is something about her I don't trust. I don't buy that shit story that she was in Quantico during the raids on Vargas. I don't believe she didn't know what that prick Alverez was doing."

"Jesus, Cafferty, give her a break. Do you tell everyone you know when you go undercover? That's the idea of 'undercover' *no one knows* about it. I'm hearing from all my sources that still talk to me that she was there learning about new tactics and surveillance."

"You seriously didn't just smart off to me did you, you little weasel?" Cafferty said a little surprised. "Okay, so the bitch is off in Quantico while Vargas's organization is being infiltrated by Alverez. Any news on who the other agent was?"

"No. Tyler is tight-lipped about it all, as is everyone else involved with the operation," Foreman answered as he ran his hand through what hair he had, all the while his thoughts on how to keep from ending up dead and keeping his career intact.

"Keep digging, Foreman. It's the only thing that's keeping me from getting rid of you," Cafferty said before turning and walking back to his car. "Oh, and by the way, Vincent says he has something for your lovely wife to try. You remember her dealer, right?" He laughed as he opened the door and slid in.

Foreman hated Cafferty. He hated that the sleazy agent was blackmailing him. He hated that his wife was hooked on drugs. And most of all, he hated that he couldn't do a damn thing about any of it. The only thing he was grateful for was the fact that his sons didn't know how bad he had fucked up. He got into his car, and the overwhelming sense that his world was crashing down on him overtook him. He broke down into tears, tears of anger, frustration, and shame. He regretted that there was nothing he could do for the love of his life; and for a brief moment the thought of taking his firearm and ending it all flashed through his mind. *You could always come clean with the agency and spill it all,* he heard the voice in his head say. *Maybe everything could turn out all right.* He could talk to SAC Sullivan, maybe plead that stress had driven him to make the comments he made. *No flippin' way are you my boss. I don't work under you. Though the thought of working over you is appealing.* "Jesus, what the hell was I thinking?" he thought. Hell, he would plead anything. There had to be some kind of deal he could work out and come out of this without doing major time and losing everything. As he pulled himself together, he said, "Yeah, don't count on it." He started his car and drove away.

✝

"I need to see you. How soon can you meet me?" Tom spoke into the phone.

"Hmm, from what I can tell I have one appointment and I should be done about one. Is that soon enough?" Michaela Benedict replied as she smiled.

"Works for me. Should I just let myself in?"

"Of course, you know where the key is."

"Good. I'll have a bottle chilling and be out by the pool, okay?"

"Looking forward to it, darling," Michaela responded as she immediately envisioned the lean, muscular body with droplets of water dripping off it. Michaela hung up the phone and tossed her pen down then stood up and grabbed her jacket and headed out the door. She stopped at the desk and said, "Rachel, reschedule my appointment, please. I'll be out of the office the rest of the day."

✝

"I seriously need some water," Michaela said as she pushed herself up and reached for the throw blanket that had worked its way to the floor. Wrapping it around her she spoke as she walked to the kitchen, "How long are you in town?"

37

"Not sure," Tom replied as he pulled his pants on and buttoned them. "I suppose it all depends on how quick I can wrap business up."

"And how is business, considering it's the only thing that brings you to town?"

"Hmm…it's enriching." Tom laughed. "Seriously, you want to talk shop?" He walked to the fridge, pulled out a bottle of water and twisted the cap off. After taking a long drink he wiped his mouth and looked at her. *What's with that comment she made? Is she getting clingy? Shit, I hope not. If she is I'm gonna have to end these little visits.*

"I was just asking. It would be nice to see you more often," she answered as she walked up to him and dragged her finger down his broad chest.

"I'll see what I can do," he said as he smiled at her.

Michaela laughed then said, "No you won't, we both know that. Did you have lunch?"

"No, I didn't. I picked up some wine and came straight here. Did you…do you want me to order some Chinese or something?"

"Are you staying?"

"Is that an invitation?"

"Up to you, I suppose. I'm gonna go rinse off then jump in the pool. Care to join?"

"Sounds like an idea, yeah, I think I will…join you in the shower and a dip in the pool sounds wonderful. It is getting pretty hot in here, isn't it?" Tom said as he tipped the bottle to his mouth again. The ringing of his cell phone drew his attention, and with an apologetic smile he pulled it from his pocket.

"Yeah, what's up?" he said into the small device. After listening to the voice on the other end he went on, "I see, and you can't handle things hence the phone call to me. Give me half an hour and I'll be there." With a push of the button he disconnected the call.

"Business calling I hear, knew it was too good to be true." Michaela laughed hiding her disappointment.

"I'm sorry, love, the price one pays for employing idiots," Tom said as he walked to his shirt and picked it up off the floor.

"Mmhmm. Just make sure the door is locked when you go out, I'm jumping in the shower. Maybe you can call again before you leave town," Michaela said as she walked past Tom toward her bedroom, leaving him alone in the living room. He slipped his shirt on and as he buttoned the last button, looked at the closed door. With a sigh he walked out the front door, making sure it was locked as he pulled it closed.

Chapter Six

Amanda walked into the hospital on her way to see Lucinda Velazquez. She opened the door to the room and quietly walked in. She wasn't at all sure what she expected to find out if Lucinda was asleep, or how she was going to identify herself, if she wasn't. She could always say she was a volunteer, would the woman believe that? Well, you can't exactly tell her the truth can you? Wait, why not? Movement from the bed drew her attention and stopped the mental argument going on in her head.

Luce focused on the woman. "Who are you?" she asked.

"Um…hi, I'm Amanda. How are you feeling, is there anything I can get you?"

"A drink of water would be great, thanks," Luce replied as she closed her eyes. Amanda went to the small table stand and poured some water. "Here you go," she said as she held the paper cup with the straw to Luce's lips.

Luce opened her eyes and took a sip from the straw. "Thanks, if you could…I can't reach the button to adjust the bed."

"Oh, um…is that a good idea?" Amanda asked as she took a step back. Luce turned her head and looked at the redhead. "Of course it is. I was sitting up earlier."

"Okay, here we go," Amanda said as she pushed the button that raised the top part of the bed to a sitting position. "Now what else can I do for you?" she said as she looked at Luce's deep blue eyes. *Oh, god, those eyes…they're amazing.*

"I think I'm good, thank you. I'm sure you have other patients that need things from you."

"Oh, it's all right, I can sit and talk if you'd like."

"That would actually be nice. The only person I've talked to has been Jessica and quite frankly she hasn't had a whole lot of good things to say lately."

"That doesn't sound good, but I'm sure she doesn't realize all she says comes across to you as bad things," Amanda said as she pulled a chair closer to the bed.

"Oh, she knows, I believe she does it on purpose; like she is making sure her point is driven home. Well, it won't work. I know for a fact that Beth loves me and isn't what Jess thinks."

"Well, what does Jess think?"

"She thinks that Beth doesn't really love me and that she is...oh, it doesn't matter. I know she is just tryin' to protect me but, still, why can't she just let me be happy, ya know?"

"I don't know. Do you think this girl, Beth, loves you?" Amanda asked.

"Well, of course I do. What kind of stupid question is that?" Luce said as she looked at the redhead as if she had lost her mind. "There are just some things you know, and I know she loves me. I can't decide if Jess just doesn't like her or if she is jealous."

Not knowing what to say, Amanda replied. "Um, well maybe she just sees something that you don't."

"I don't know, but why would she be jealous? It's not like we can revisit that again, right?"

"Well, I don't know. I suppose it all depends on if you want to or not, don't you think?" Amanda asked as she sat back in her chair and watched Luce.

"It doesn't matter. Like I said I love Beth and she loves me. So what did you say your name is?" Luce replied as she tried to recall the woman's name.

"Amanda."

"Yes, that's right, Amanda…so tell me what has you sitting with me listening to me complain about trivial crap."

"Um, well I came in to make sure you were all right. I was just about to leave when you woke up." Amanda found the words coming out of her mouth without even thinking. *Okay, I guess we aren't going with the truth.*

"Yeah, but why did you stay?" Luce asked as her blue eyes pierced Amanda.

"I don't know, I suppose I felt like you wanted to talk. If I was wrong, I apologize," Amanda replied.

"I'm sorry. I'm just so damn tired of being in this bed…of being here, not being able to do anything."

"I can understand that, but remember you're here for a reason. You need to give your body time to heal."

With a roll of her eyes, Luce asked, "Can you find out when I can get up and at least walk around?" Luce fidgeted as she tried to get comfortable.

"Of course, let me see if I can find the doctor," Amanda said as she stood. "Is there anything I can get you before I go?" she asked.

"Nope, I'll be fine," Luce spoke as the redhead walked to the door. Amanda opened the door then stopped and glanced back at Luce one last time before she left. *Okay, I could find myself in trouble here if I don't watch myself,* Amanda thought as she walked down the hall. She reached her car and just sat and thought for a while after she got in. She thought of what Luce had told her and thought about how she was going to work this into a story. Hell was there even a story? Something in her gut was screaming there was, and her gut was never wrong. Maybe she would return later and use the same 'volunteer' cover. With a plan made, she started her car and headed toward her office.

†

Luce had closed her eyes as soon as Amanda walked out and the next time she opened them, the doctor was looking over her chart. "What's the verdict, Doc, am I gonna make it?" Luce joked.

"It does appear so, young lady, although you gave a few people a good scare. Everything is looking good. You mind if I take a look?" he asked as he set the clipboard down and walked toward the right side of the bed.

"No, not at all, maybe you can tell me when I can get up and walk around. I asked Amanda to find out for me and well, she must have gotten busy."

"Oh, that looks real good," the doctor said as he examined the surgical site. "It's healing quite well. I think if you can handle walking up and down the hallway, you should be able to leave this place in…oh I'd say a few more days. How's that sound to you?"

"Are you serious? That sounds fantastic! Can I get up now and try walkin' the place?" Luce asked excitedly.

"Can you take it slow?" the doctor asked with a smile on his face. "Let me get a nurse to help you okay, hang tight she will be in shortly." The doctor wrote notes in the chart he had picked up again. Luce's mood was much improved and she found it hard to contain her smile. She was so tired of being stuck in this bed. "Uh, doc, before you go can you hand me the phone, I'd like to make a call." The doctor smiled and handed her the phone.

With the phone in her hand and the doctor closing the door, Luce dialed Jessica's number. "Hey, wanna come walk with me?" she said as soon as Jessica answered.

"Want to tell me what you're talking about? Last I heard you're stuck in bed."

"Nope, just saw the doc and he said if I can handle walking up and down the hall I can leave this damned place. So get your ass over here as soon as you can," Luce said.

"And you being you have to do that this very instant, right?" Jessica said, smiling as she glanced over the paper in her hand. She could just imagine Luce chomping at the bit to get up and get back to work. This meant that it wouldn't take her long to start looking for Beth.

"Well, yeah. I'm tired of this bed, of this room, of this place. So get here soon okay?"

"Yeah, I'll be there soon, just keep your pants on. Oh wait, you aren't wearing any pants!" Jessica laughed.

"Yeah, you might wanna bring me some so I have something to wear home; the key is still under the potted plant by the door."

"Yeah, I'll be there soon as I can wrap up some things here, okay?"

"Great." Luce said with a smile then hung up the phone.

Jessica sat back as she looked at the receiver she held in her hand. "Shit, now what? She is gonna start looking for that damn woman. Doesn't mean she'll find her though," she said as she tapped the receiver on her chin and thought.

†

The next few days Jessica pored over more files as Luce adjusted to being at home and easing herself back into work with a few hours here and a few hours there. For Luce it wasn't what she was used to, but it was better than lying in a bed in some hospital; plus it gave her time to look for Beth.

Luce was standing at the water cooler when she heard a voice behind her ask, "Excuse me, I was wondering if you could tell me where I might find a…Lucinda Velazquez?"

"Is she expecting you?" Luce asked as she stood up and turned, only to find she was looking at the hospital volunteer.

"No, she isn't," Amanda replied as she looked up from her notebook and found herself looking into deep blue eyes. "Uh, well, hi there."

"Yeah, hi there. Amanda right?"

"Yeah…um, I suppose I owe you an apology for never having gotten you that walk the other day. You look like you're getting along well."

"Yeah, I'm doing fine I suppose…so, uh, what can I do for you? I'm up and moving and this isn't the hospital," Luce asked as she brought the paper cup to her mouth.

"Um…I need to tell you I'm not a hospital volunteer, I'm really a reporter. My name is Amanda Murphy. I know this sounds strange, but I got a call a few days ago that suggested I look into the death of Judge Marcus Stone. More to the point they suggested I focus on Beth Ryan and Donavon Vargas. I've read the police reports and nothing is ever mentioned about either of them."

"Okay and you came to me why?"

"Well, Vargas was a drug dealer, you're DEA…it wasn't too much of a leap to wonder if you know anything."

"Really…somehow I find that too easy of an explanation."

"I read up on Vargas. He was killed in a park where an agent was also shot. I spoke with Agent Tyler. When he said he couldn't comment on anything I followed him to the hospital."

"Well, I'm sorry you wasted your time, I don't know anything. Now if you'll excuse me I have some work to get caught up on," Luce said as she turned to walk away.

"No, please hear me out," Amanda spoke as she followed Luce.

"Honestly, I can't help you…not that I would even if I could."

"Why? Okay look, I know that you have feelings for this woman that is if she is the same Beth you spoke of the other day, but if that's the case wouldn't you want to clear her name?"

"Look, I don't have time for all of this, and I don't have time to deal with you. Go play reporter or volunteer or whatever it is you do somewhere else and leave me the hell alone," Luce said as she walked into Jessica's office and shut the door leaving the redhead standing in the hallway. "Well, that worked well," Amanda said under her breath.

†

Jessica looked up with confusion on her face as the door closed. "Is there something I can do for you?" she asked Luce.

"Yeah, do you know if anyone is looking at Beth as a suspect in the death of a judge by the name of Marcus Stone?" Luce asked as she placed her hands on her hips, a frown on her face.

With a frown creasing her forehead Jessica placed the pen she held in her hand on the desk and sat back. "What?" she asked.

"I was just approached by a reporter who told me she received a tip about a link between Beth, Vargas, and this judge. You got any idea what that's all about?"

"No, none…tell me exactly what she said," Jessica said, leaning forward and placing her elbows on her desk.

Pulling up a chair Luce sat down. "Amanda Murphy. I woke up the other morning to find this redhead in my room. She pretended to be a nurse volunteer, and she just showed up here asking for me. She then proceeded to tell me about a tip she received on Beth. Now I'm asking you if you know anything about that."

"Why the hell would I know anything about that?"

"Well, maybe because you're here on some investigation. I figure maybe that has something to do with it."

"Yeah, about the reason I'm here, it's a long story and it's been a long day, how about we go grab a bite to eat and catch up," Jessica said as she stood up, closing the open file on her desk. Together they walked out of the building discussing all the possibilities for dinner. Settling on their old favorite Irish pub Jessica got in her car and Luce walked to hers.

Luce wondered if she should speak with Amanda Murphy. *Why wouldn't you speak with her, it's not like you're gonna screw her.* "Whoa, where did that thought come from," she asked herself, shocked that she had even subconsciously considered bedding the redhead. "Okay, so it's been a long time, and it's not like I even know where Beth is; of course I'm going to think about sex once in a while, and face it, the woman is gorgeous. Yeah, and you're the faithful one, right?" Her subconscious voice spoke as she shut the door to her car and started it up to follow Jessica. Damn right she was faithful. She never screwed around when she was with someone, but was she really with Beth? In all honestly, Beth was god knows where, doing god knows what. That alone made it hard to have any sort of relationship. *Jesus, Luce, get a grip.* Luce brought her thoughts back to a more comfortable level; she wasn't dealing well with not knowing where Beth was and not being with her. Realizing she was at her destination, she pulled into the parking lot. Jessica was waiting for her and together they walked into the establishment and were quickly seated. The food was excellent, atmosphere homey, and when live music was available it was good, so it never took long for the place to fill. The mix of light chatter and music from the other room soon had them relaxing with a mug of beer. "So tell me, is Amanda Murphy as pretty as her picture makes her out to be?"

"Yeah, I suppose she could be considered pretty. I don't know, I really didn't pay that much attention to her," Luce replied as she took a sip of her beer.

"Oh, come on, you expect me to believe that? I know you, remember. If a woman has a pulse you notice," Jessica said with a bit more venom than she intended.

Ignoring the tone Luce said, "I don't cheat."

"You're right, you don't. But you know there is a big difference between appreciating and cheating. How do you know Beth is being just as noble and honorable as you are?"

"Well, that, my friend, is something I'd think you would know. After all you have the connections to know where she is, what and who she is doing, right," Luce replied as she sat back, a trace of anger in her voice.

Jessica closed her eyes for a moment before responding. "Luce, how many ways do I need to say this: I don't know where Beth is. I didn't know they were taking her into the witness protection program." *Shit, it's not going to be pretty when she finds out I just lied to her.*

"What do you have against Beth, why don't you like her?" Luce asked.

"Where did that come from?" Jessica asked, a bit taken aback.

"I just…I don't know. You don't like her; I can tell just by the way you talk about her, the way you behave when her name comes up."

"Look, it's that I can't help you. I'm sorry. I in no way meant that to show as dislike toward her."

"Can't…right," Luce repeated, sarcastically.

"Stop it. I can't…I don't know what you want me to do here."

"Help me. You have contacts that could help you find her. If you really don't know where she is, you know people that do. Mine don't have the reach yours do."

"Honestly, Luce, I don't. I'm tired of arguing with you about it. So tell me why you didn't want to talk with the reporter?" Jessica asked, hoping to change the subject.

"Because it's AMANDA MURPHY, you know her reputation as well as I do. She is like a bulldog; once she gets a hold of something she doesn't let go. I don't want to be the bone she won't let go of," Luce spoke as she sat back in her chair.

"Maybe she just wants to get to know the intriguing Lucinda Velazquez," Jessica said as she began to laugh.

Luce who had just taken a drink of beer began to cough as she swallowed hard and laughed. "Intriguing? What the hell…sexy, hot, wildly all-consuming, maybe," she replied before she started laughing. When their waitress arrived a minute later, Jessica caught her breath and said, "Okay, tiger, back to reality, it's time to order." Looking at the cute, short-haired waitress, Jessica said, "I believe I'll have the shepherd's pie." As the waitress wrote the two flirted over what went best with it as far as side dishes. Finally Luce spoke up and joined in the conversation. Once they had both placed their orders and the waitress, whose name Jessica found out was Lauren, had left, the conversation returned to Beth. "So have you found anything more about Beth's past?"

"Why so interested?" Luce responded as she sat forward to look intently into her friend's eyes.

"Because she is important to you, that's why. Look, I know you feel like I am pushing for her to be guilty of something, but I'm really not. I just want you to have all the facts. I wasn't for her going into protective custody, but honestly it is the best place for her. I really am in your corner."

"Wait, you said you had no idea she was going into witness protection."

"I didn't know. Look, all I'm trying to say is that it is the best place for her," Jessica said.

"For some reason I don't believe you. Anyway no one wants to talk about her after they find out I'm a fed. And now what am I supposed to do with this Judge Stone mess? You know they'll clam up even tighter now." Luce thought about the numerous phone calls she had made during the last couple of days. Since she couldn't be out in the field and was still technically on leave she had plenty of time; time she decided to use to find Beth.

"I wonder…just hear me out, okay. Maybe someone that loves digging would be useful, someone like, say, Amanda Murphy?" Jessica said as she waited for the blowup.

"I just heard you wrong, would you mind repeating that?" Luce spoke, her voice quiet and low.

"Ms. Murphy. She showed up asking to speak with you today. You said yourself just a bit ago that she is like a bulldog. We set her on the trail of Beth's past and see what she turns up, of course with our help that is…"

"No."

"Okay, it's your call," Jessica said just as their order appeared. "Oh, wow, this looks great. I can imagine your boyfriend loves when you serve him something like this!" she said as she smiled at Lauren.

"I would hope the one I'm with would love it when I serve them," the woman said with a huge smile of her own. "And here is your dinner," she said as she barely glanced at Luce. With her eyes going back to Jessica she once again gave a smile and said, "If there is *anything* you would like, please don't hesitate."

"You can bet I'll give a shout."

"What if I need something?" Luce asked as she teased the woman as well.

"Well, I suppose I could see what I could work out for you. Can I get you anything else?" Lauren asked. After a little more flirting from Jessica, who told her they were fine for the moment, she left to handle the rest of her customers.

"Damn, she is all of what twenty years old?" Luce remarked.

"Looks old enough to me," Jessica replied as she turned to watch the woman in question as she moved around to the different tables. Luce was right. The woman was young, but hell she was of age and giving Jessica all the signs that gave her the go-ahead. Besides it wasn't like Jessica was tied to anyone, never mind the fact that she was a good ten to fifteen years older than Lauren. *Shit age doesn't matter really.*

"What's up with you?" Luce asked as she watched her friend.

"What do you mean?" Jessica said before placing a forkful of ground lamb and veggies with a dab of whipped potatoes into her mouth. She did not want to have this conversation.

"Well, you've been in town for, what, about a month and a half, and we really haven't been able to just sit and catch up with each other, so…what's up?"

"Oh, yeah, well you know if you would keep your ass out of trouble we wouldn't have been so preoccupied when I got into town."

"True, I suppose that would have made a bit of a difference, but hey you know me, have to keep things lively!"

"Lively? Seriously, you took a bullet in the chest that just barely missed your heart, got involved with a drug lord's girl, and watched Joe be killed. That's more like standing on the edge of a knife trying not to fall and be split in half."

"Yeah, well, things can't always be on an even keel," Luce joked dryly. "And stop changing the subject, you're supposed to be telling me what's going on in your life and with you. Don't get me wrong, I'm glad as hell you showed up when you did, but what brought you to town?" Luce asked as she motioned the waitress for another round of drinks.

"My life, hmm, well, it has its ups and downs, and what brings me here is shoptalk, and while I thought I wanted to get into it tonight, I think I've changed my mind. Do you honestly want shoptalk?" Jessica said as she thought about the evasive answer to events in her life. *Luce isn't gonna let you slip with that one,* the little voice in her head said.

"Later, you're being secretive about *you,* what's up?" Luce said as she pushed her plate away and leaned forward with her elbows resting on the table, her hands clasped in front of her, her chin inches away from them.

"God, where do you want me to start?"

"How about last time I saw you. You had just received a job offer from Phoenix and you were thinking about taking it, no matter what Gloria said, then puff you're gone, she is left here and I don't hear from you in how long?"

"Jesus, let it go. I had my reasons, and maybe they were wrong but lessons learned, right?"

"I'm sorry. I shouldn't have brought that up, it's in the past and that's where it should stay."

"I thought we had moved past that?" Jessica said as she remembered that time long ago.

"We did. I guess I was just surprised to hear your voice in the morgue the night Joe died. How did you know I was there?"

"Business...I walked into Tyler's office just as all hell was breaking loose; he filled me in and as he was finishing up, he was told that they had you secure and that they had recovered Joe's body. Luce...I didn't want to get into this here, but it seems like it's gonna happen anyway. I've been assigned by my bosses to work with Douglas Tyler. We were alerted to some things that need looking into."

"Like what?" Luce asked as she took another drink and thought.

"I knew I shouldn't have said anything. How about you think about what I just told you and we save the rest of it for tomorrow, okay? For now, let's just enjoy each other's company and relax some." Jessica sat back and caught Lauren watching them and with a smile she acknowledged the woman, who walked toward them.

"So are you two ready for dessert?" The five foot three blond, blued-eyed woman asked as she flashed Jessica a flirtatious smile.

"Well, maybe if you told us what you have you could entice us," Luce replied as she took advantage of Jessica's misfortune of just having taken a last bite of her dinner.

Turning toward Luce, and dropping the flirtatious smile down to a friendly one, Lauren listed several items, including a mocha cake, which Luce jumped at. Jessica went with a slice of apple pie, which Lauren swore was almost as good as hers. With a light touch to Jessica's shoulder she took off to the kitchen to bring the desserts.

"Seriously, what am I, chopped liver?" Luce asked, looking a tad put off that the woman had dismissed her attempt at flirting. *What the hell, why does it matter to me that she isn't falling all over me,* she wondered. With a laugh Jessica sat back in her seat and asked, "You are not jealous, are you?"

"Ha, not even…well, no, why would I be? Jesus, I sound like I am, don't I," Luce replied, turning slightly red with embarrassment.

"Oh, my god, you are!" Jessica said, astonishment in her voice. "What is going on with you?" she asked as she sat forward. Just as Luce was about to answer, their dessert arrived. "I don't know," Luce answered when the woman walked away. "I guess I'm missing Beth more than I thought."

"Is that all?" Jessica asked, truly concerned. "I don't think I've ever known you to be jealous of anyone."

"That's because I haven't been."

"Then why now?"

"Hell, I don't know," Luce said a little more forcefully than she meant to. "Shit, I'm sorry. I don't know. She is making me feel like I'm invisible…"

"Who is?" Jessica asked.

"Lauren…" Luce answered her tone a bit on the bitchy side.

"Uh, okay, this is a bit out of the *Twilight Zone*. She isn't even your type, and, as you pointed out earlier, you're taken.

Since when do you need every woman you interact with to fall at your feet?"

"I don't…I don't know. Like I said, I'm just missing Beth more than I thought," Luce said, ready to put this conversation aside. *What is going on…is Jess right? Lauren isn't my type at all. Come on, you know what's going on. You're pissed off that someone is showing interest in Jessica,* her little voice said. *No, that is not it.* She looked up to see Jessica watching her. "What?"

"Nothing, it's just that I've never seen this side of you…I suppose it surprises me," Jessica said. *No don't go there; this has nothing to do with you,* her little voice said. *It could,* she answered back.

"So are you staying at Tom's while you're here?" Luce asked, changing the subject.

"Yeah, damn good thing he doesn't mind me taking over his place once in a while," Jessica replied as she thought about her brother.

"Bet he likes having you around, well, when you're actually around. No, wait, he isn't in town is he? At least I don't remember him being around that night after I told Rebecca about Joe," Luce said as she vaguely recalled that night not so long ago.

"No, he was out of the country on some African safari. He got back a few days ago. He was supposed to stop and see you while you were at the hospital, I take it he didn't."

"Wow, he must be doing something right! No, he didn't. I'm sure he had more pressing things to attend to, like some hot young woman," Luce said with a smile as she thought about Jessica's younger brother.

Tom Sullivan, like his older sister, had black hair, ice-blue eyes, and her sense of humor, and that was about all. He, like Jessica, had received a decent inheritance from their grandfather, and while she placed hers into stocks and bonds, no one was really sure what he had done with his share. The one thing they did know was he wasn't lacking for money and he came and went as he pleased.

"Granddaddy would be so ashamed if he knew how Tom spends his time," Jessica said softly. "So would Mom actually."

"Is he in trouble with law enforcement?"

"No."

"Is he under surveillance by anyone?"

"Not that I know of, what's your point here, Luce?"

"My point is he is just a young man sowing his oats. He has the funds why not?" Luce asked as she sat back and glanced at the stage and the band members.

"Okay, you have a point, but Granddaddy and Mom wanted him to accomplish something with his life, and he isn't."

"You don't know that. When was the last time you actually spent any real time with him?" Luce asked as she brought her eyes back to the woman seated across from her, her eyes boring into her.

"You're right, but tell me, what do *you* think he does for money since he doesn't work? And please don't tell me you think he was smart and made some real good investments. Tommy was never good with what money he earned, much less money he was given," Jessica replied, not truly wanting to think about what her brother did for money.

"Look, I know a long time ago he ran real close to the edge of breaking the law. Hell, I'd hazard a guess that we all did to some degree; but, I work here, I have ties to all the law enforcement offices around, and not once has there been anything in the air about him. I honestly think you're just looking for things to worry about here."

"Why the hell would I do that, Luce?" Jessica asked.

"I don't know. Are you looking for some reason to come back? You think he needs taken care of so if you swoop back into town to watch out for him you have reason and all is good."

"God, you're so full of shit!" Jessica exclaimed. "I don't want to come back, not that I'd need a reason if I did."

Chapter Seven

Amanda Murphy had had a long day and all she wanted was a good Irish beer, a decent meal, and some music. So when she entered Nagy's she was ready to let her hair down. She was led to a booth where she placed her order for an Irish Red and left to look over the menu. The chatter and laughter combined with music worked to relax her, and as she glanced around the room her eyes caught two very striking women. "Are you ready to order, sweetie?" the waitress asked as she pushed her hair behind her ear and smiled.

Amanda broke into a big smile when she looked up and saw her waitress was Sylvia. The two had dated briefly and parted dear friends. "I think I'll go with the fish and chips."

"Good choice, can I get you anything else? Some dessert maybe or do you want to wait and see how you're feeling later?"

"I'll wait, thank you."

"Great. I'll get this in for you. You came in on a good night. I think you'll like the band. They are good."

"They sound great. What time are you off, Sylvia?" Amanda said with a smile.

"I'll be off at ten. What do you have in mind?"

"Oh, I don't know, get you off those feet for sure; from there the sky's the limit," Amanda replied.

"What would you actually do if I ever took you up on that? I'll be back with your dinner, okay, sweetie? Need another beer too?"

"Probably freak the fuck out; and yeah, might as well," Amanda said with a wink. Once Sylvia left, her eyes went back to the table that had drawn her attention earlier. Amanda was comfortable with the flirtatious banter that existed between herself and Sylvia. She knew Sylvia was devoted to her partner, and well, she was married to her job. Her attention went back to the two women until her phone rang and without much consideration she answered. "Amanda Murphy here," she spoke.

"Hey, Amanda, how's it going?"

"Been a long day, my friend, what about you?" she asked Ron.

"Same. So did you catch up with that DEA agent?"

"She won't talk yet, but she will by the time I'm done," she said as her eyes went back to the table and the topic of their discussion.

"Oh, I'm sure she will. Listen, I did some digging on Judge Stone."

"Great, what's the story?"

"Judge Marcus Ray Stone died at the age of sixty during a home invasion. According to police reports, neighbors reported hearing gunshots around two in the morning. When police arrived, the front door was open. They entered and found the judge lying in his office, dead from a single shot to the head. Safe was open as well as the desk drawers. His wife was out of town, visiting her sister. She said the judge had money in the safe as well as some old coins."

"Were there any leads on the shooter?" Amanda asked as she smiled and nodded at Luce, who had just looked in her direction.

"No, nothing. No one saw a thing."

"Okay, did the coins ever turn up?" she asked.

"Nothing yet..."

"That's interesting, who steals old coins and holds on to them?"

"I don't know, someone who collects them?"

"I don't see a collector breaking in and shooting the homeowner and taking money do you?"

"I don't know, weird shit happens every day."

"I don't know, doesn't feel right to me. Look, my dinner just arrived so I'll touch base with you tomorrow, okay?" Amanda said as Sylvia approached the table.

"Sounds good, have a good night, Mandy."

†

"Oh shit, I have the worst luck known to man," Luce spoke as she looked back at Jessica.

"Why?" Jessica said confused as to why Luce would just say that out of the clear blue sky.

"The reporter is here," Luce answered.

"Will you relax, just because she is here doesn't mean she will come to talk to you."

"Okay, you have a point." She had just finished speaking those words when she felt a hand on her shoulder, and as she turned her head she saw the beautiful green eyes of the woman they had been talking about.

"Hello, imagine meeting you here." Amanda turned to look at Jessica. "Hi, I'm Amanda Murphy," she said in a friendly tone as she extended her right hand to Jessica.

Jessica extended her hand as she spoke, "Nice to meet you."

"I just saw you sitting here and wanted to say hello and apologize again for the way we met the other day."

"Nothing to apologize for, it was my fault for assuming you were with the hospital," Luce said as she looked up at Amanda.

With a big smile Amanda said, "Well, I didn't mean to interrupt your dinner. I just wanted to come and say hi. Maybe we can speak tomorrow; I'd still like to discuss that matter with you."

"Tell me again why you believe I can help you?"

"Honestly, until recently, I thought it was a complete waste of time. But now, my gut is telling me there's something here, and I think you're involved. My gut tells me you were involved with the shooting that ended Vargas's life. Look, I'm sorry, I've taken enough of your time, so I'll let you two go back to your conversation and dinner. Jessica, it was nice to meet you. Luce, I hope to see you again tomorrow. I'll swing by the offices and we can talk more."

"Nice to meet you as well," Jessica said as she smiled at Amanda before she turned and walked back to her own table. "She doesn't come across as scary, why don't you meet with her?"

"I knew you were gonna say that, damn it. I just don't want to. Is my name connected with Vargas in any way? I am supposed to be in the shadows; there are still crewmembers out there looking for my fucking head!" Luce said, her voice slowly increasing in intensity.

"Hey, calm down, this isn't the place to lose it," Jessica said as she sat forward and reached for Luce's hand. "Come on, let's get out of here." She motioned for Lauren to bring their bill. With a sigh she stood up and ushered her friend out of the restaurant.

✝

Waking up early, Luce enjoyed the early morning sun, which was casting various shades of reds and oranges with a few purples tossed in, and made for a breathtaking picture. It never failed to astound Luce and made her feel so lucky to be alive, which was a big difference from not so long ago. While she never consciously considered killing herself, she wasn't exactly caring about being alive either. *God I was really in a bad place,* she thought as she set out for an early morning walk, it was usually a run, but she was still working up to that since her release from the hospital a week and a half ago.

Some thirty minutes later Luce did some light stretches hoping to alleviate some of the discomfort from her muscles, which weren't as bad as they had been the previous days. With a little luck, the doctor assured her, it wouldn't be long before she was back to running her usual distance and speed, and then she would be able to get back in the field instead of desk duty. Returning home from her workout she grabbed a small towel off the kitchen counter and wiped the sweat from her face. Making her way to the shower, she stripped off her running clothes and dropped them in a pile along with the towel. After the quick shower, she dried off and wrapped a towel around her then went in search of coffee.

With a steaming cup of the dark, heavenly liquid in hand, she walked to her bedroom and pulled out a pair of boxers, a pair of well-worn Levi's, bra, and black tee. Once dressed, she slipped on socks and then her boots. As she took the final drink from her cup, she glanced at the clock on her bedside stand and grabbed her clip-on holster and her badge. She went to the kitchen to drop off her cup then to the side door leading to the garage. With the touch of a button, the garage door opened and she slid into her new Dodge Avenger. The turn of the key fired the engine up and she backed out of her driveway, music piping out of the car speakers. Not liking the song Luce switched the station and was taken immediately to a favorite station, which played a mix of everything from Ozzy to Nickelback, to an occasional love song. At the moment a favorite from way back when was playing. She immediately began singing along with Bret Michaels, who sang about *"nothing but a good time."* She remembered the parties and clubs, dancing with the girls who couldn't wait to spend a few minutes with her. "Damn those were good times," she said as the song ended. The run and the music put her in a good mood, and she couldn't wait to get the day going. She pulled into a Starbucks drive-through and ordered a low-fat latte. Singing along with the radio, Luce drove toward the office and by the time she arrived at her desk she was whistling.

†

On the other side of town, Jessica wasn't having a morning even remotely close to Luce's experience. Jessica woke up with a hangover and Lauren lying next to her. As she rubbed her face and searched her foggy mind for memories of the night before, she felt a warm hand gliding over her taut stomach. *Oh shit, what did I do?* she asked herself.

"Mm, good morning sexy," Lauren spoke softly.

"Uh, good morning." *Thomas, please don't be home, I really don't want to deal with your shit-eating grin.* "Want some coffee?" Jessica asked as she got out of bed and walked to the chair where her robe laid then headed for the master bath to brush her teeth.

"That sounds great," Lauren answered as she got up and followed Jessica. Jessica was in the process of rinsing her mouth when she felt the blond woman walk up behind her and kiss her shoulder. "Here is an extra toothbrush," Jessica said as she opened a drawer and grabbed one. She pulled away and left the room to go make coffee. *Shit, I knew I shouldn't have gone back to the pub last night,* she thought as she opened a cupboard and grabbed a bottle of aspirin.

The coffee had just stopped brewing when Lauren, dressed but barefoot, walked into the kitchen. Jessica reached for two coffee cups and began pouring. "Do you need cream and sugar?" she asked.

"No, black is fine, thank you." Lauren sat on the stool next to the counter and watched the other woman, then softly said, "You can relax; it was just sex, that doesn't equate into a relationship."

"What?" Jessica said a bit surprised.

"Last night…you don't have to be so worked up about it. I enjoyed it, I like you, and I had a good time, but it isn't anything more than that," Lauren said with a small smile when she saw Jessica relax just a fraction.

"I'm sorry. I suppose I've been behaving a little like a bitch, huh?" she said as she offered a cup to the blonde.

"A little bit," Lauren replied as her smile broadened. "Not used to sharing your space, are you?"

"It shows, huh? I haven't been involved with anyone in I can't remember how long," Jessica said as she thought about the last real involvement she had.

"Why is that? You're fun, smart, beautiful…I'm sorry, I shouldn't have asked, way out of line there," Lauren said as she blushed and took a sip of coffee to hide her discomfort.

"I guess partly the job; maybe I'm afraid of commitment…I don't know," Jessica answered, trying to be light with the answer but striking a nerve in her. *Be serious, you know damn well it isn't the job, and commitment isn't the issue either.*

"Ah, so what is your job, by the way," Lauren asked.

With a smile, Jessica sat on the other stool and relaxed a tad more. "I work for the ATF."

"Wow, that sounds exciting!" Lauren exclaimed.

"Not really," Jessica answered as she smiled and lifted the cup to her lips.

"How can it not be? I mean, I realize it's dangerous and all, but still!"

"Honestly, it's just a lot of paperwork that can be very tedious at times."

"So there's no travel to exotic locations to shoot it out with the bad guys, huh. Well that's good, because I would hate the thought of anything bad happening to you in the line of duty," Lauren said.

"I try to stay out of gunfights," Jessica replied as her thoughts traveled to the not so long ago when she barely missed the firefight between Donavon Vargas and Luce. It was about two weeks after she got back into town. Vargas and a couple of other men had been arrested. On his way to a court hearing, Vargas managed to escape. It became apparent that Vargas had men tracking Beth Ryan. Thinking back, it was a miracle that she remembered Luce telling her she'd planned to go to that park. She and officers of the police force arrived shortly before the shootout. Shaking the memories she asked, "Need more coffee?"

"No, I should be going," Lauren replied as she stood up and took her cup to the sink. "Thank you for a fantastic time, maybe we can do it again."

With a slight smile Jessica set her cup down and stood as well. As she walked her guest to the door, she simply said, "Maybe. You never know what will happen."

Laughing, Lauren said, "Remember, it is what it is, nothing more nothing less. I enjoyed myself and I hope you did as well. I'm thinking from the intensity of the few screams I heard, you did." With a wink, Lauren placed a kiss on Jessica's cheek and left. Left staring out of her doorway down the now empty hallway, Jessica felt a small amount of relief at Lauren's words. Closing the door and heading for the shower, Jessica thought about the reasons she hadn't been in any serious relationship. It was true that being involved with a federal agent took a special kind of person, but there were plenty of special women in the world and she had the privilege of knowing a few of them, so that wasn't the issue. Neither was being afraid of commitment. She has been at the same job for how many years now? If it had been a matter of commitment, she would have left the job a long time ago considering all she had seen and had to deal with. *Come on,*

Jess, you know damn well what the problem is, her conscience said, leaving her to utter "Shut the fuck up," as she threw the robe on the floor and stepped into the shower stall.

†

The shower had not helped her mood one bit. The occasional one-night stand didn't bother her, after all everyone needed someone occasionally. What bothered her was that she made an effort to make sure the other person was an adult. That wasn't to say that Lauren wasn't of age because she was. But Christ, the last time Jessica had been interested in a twenty-year-old…*she* was a twenty-year-old. To Jessica, that felt like a lifetime ago. She snorted at the memories. She and Luce had been young, had so many plans and dreams, hell they had a lifetime, right? *We should have had a lifetime. What I wouldn't give to have a second chance, I'd do so many things differently.* She had just pulled into the parking garage of the building that housed the ATF field office and into her parking spot when a song started to play. The strains of the opening instantly took her back in time. Roberta Flack sang about seeing the sunrise in someone's eyes and her heart ached. She knew exactly how that felt. The memories were so vivid she swore if she tried, she could reach out and touch them. And at this precise moment, she didn't have the patience or energy to deal with them. In a move born out of that frustration she reached over and stabbed at the power button of the radio, killing the song immediately. With a cleansing breath, she attempted to put distance between the past and present. She got out of her truck, slammed the door shut and as she walked away, pressed the lock button on the key fob. At the same time, she desperately tried to push the memories back into the tidy, locked area in both her brain and heart from which they came.

†

Luce had been in the office long before her usual hour. She had given a lot of thought to what Jessica had said about having someone else doing the question asking where Beth was concerned. She didn't like it, but maybe Amanda would be useful. Luce got up and walked the couple of doors to the office where Jessica's office assistant sat. "Is SAC Sullivan in?"

"Not yet, can I give her a message?"

"No…" Luce replied, turning to leave then changing her mind. "Um, actually, if you could just buzz me when she does get in, I'd appreciate it," Luce said as she turned to leave again.

Walking back to her desk, her thoughts were on Beth and how to prove Jessica wrong about her. She hated that Jessica seemed hell-bent on Beth being involved in Vargas's organization. Of course, finding out that the best friend you've ever had hates your girlfriend isn't something you're supposed to like. In Luce's mind, the timeline didn't fit. Okay, yes, there was a slim possibility that Beth knew things about the organization. After all she was with Vargas, had been intimate with him and there was always pillow talk. Having Jess doubt Beth was one thing, but now there was Amanda talking about the death of a federal judge and Beth's involvement. That was something very different. She had been searching for information all morning about Beth and her relationship with the judge and kept hitting brick walls. "Why is that?" Luce asked as she picked up the file on the judge's death for what seemed like the millionth time. She had read the damned thing so many times she could recite it from memory. Still, she couldn't find anything that would prove innocence or guilt. "God, this is so fucking frustrating!" she growled as she threw the file on the desk.

"What's up? Maggie said you were looking for me," Jessica asked as she opened the door. "From the looks of it, it isn't making you happy," she finished as she walked in and closed the door behind her.

"Well, yeah, it's not, and good morning to you too."

"What's up? If you just want to talk I don't have time, I have a shitload of leads to follow."

"Wow, you're in a mood. Wake up on the wrong side of the bed or what?" Luce joked.

"Yes, as a matter of fact, I did. What did you want, Lucinda?"

As the thought dawned on her Luce said, "Oh shit, you didn't…the waitress, seriously. She is what all of nineteen?"

"Give it a rest, Luce, she is old enough."

"Okay, hey, I'm sorry I didn't mean to… Look, I have been thinking about what you said about working with Amanda Murphy. I think maybe you have a good point. People see my badge, hear me say I work for the DEA and they totally shut down on me. I need someone that can get people to talk."

"Good, about time you decide to listen to me. Have you contacted her yet?"

"No, not yet. I thought I would give her a chance to look me up again."

"Okay, well, keep me posted all right," Jessica said as she stood up from the chair she had sat down in.

"Jess…friend to friend, what's up? You're not your usual self today."

"I've just been…it was a long night, okay, and not just because of… Jesus, why am I even talking about this? I don't owe you an explanation. Shit…" Jessica said as she stormed out the door and slammed it behind her.

†

The flash of the heel and the curve of the leg caught Luce more off guard, than the tap on the desk and the smoky voice that spoke to her. The combination caused an immediate warm feeling in the pit of her being. It was the clearing of the throat that brought her back to her senses.

"I'm sorry…" she began to say before she was cut off.

"For making me feel a little bit flattered by the mini moan you just let out?"

Feeling the red creep up her neck Luce hung her head. "Oh shit, I'm uh…yeah, I'm sorry about that. I'm sorry," she repeated. "I just… Have a seat, Ms. Murphy," Luce said as she sat back down.

"Thank you," Amanda replied as she sat back and smiled again. "Like I told you last night, I'd like to talk with you about that tip I got. First off, I'd like to tell you that no one has actually named you in connection to Vargas. It's just me trying to connect the dots. And try as I might, I can't find a single thing that ties you to either Vargas or Ryan. So, I'm leaning toward this whole thing being a runaround. But then again there is that annoying little coincidence of your girlfriend's name…I wonder if it's all just that, a coincidence, " Amanda said as she sat forward.

"So this is just a fishing expedition?"

"I suppose you could look at it that way. I do want to tell you that whatever you say here is between you and I until you're ready for me to tell your story."

"You're assuming there is a story to tell. Say there is, there's always the matter of what if I'm never ready; what happens then?"

"Well, if that's the case then I walk away without a story, but having met someone who is, from all I read, a very amazing person."

"Hmm, just what have you read and where," Luce asked.

"Seems that you are a decorated officer of the law. I think I read something about you receiving a medal of valor?"

Amanda answered as she pushed back a wayward strand of her hair.

"Wow, you did do some digging, that was a while back."

"Yes, well, there wasn't anything recent, so I decided to do some real investigative journalism and do my own legwork. Figured I'd find more if I came directly to the source."

"I see," Luce spoke as she pushed her seat back and stood up. "I'm starved how about you?"

"Are you suggesting we have lunch together?" Amanda asked as she sat back, surprised. From the conversation they had the night before, she had totally gotten the feeling that Lucinda wanted nothing to do with her.

"Yeah, why not?" Luce asked. "Oh yeah, last night…look, I'm sorry about that. I can't really explain my actions or my mood. I suppose I was a little surprised to see you at the pub. I was a bit unnerved."

"I hope you didn't think I was following you."

"Come on, I'm hungry," Luce said as she reached out to help Amanda up. "What would you like to eat? I know a great little place that serves fantastic Mexican food not far from here."

"Oh, hey, is it that little place down on Tomlinson Road?"

"Yeah, you know it?" Luce teased as she pushed the front door of the building open for the cute redhead. She let her eyes drop to the well-formed ass as it swayed in front of her. *Damned nice sight isn't it*, the tiny voice deep inside her head whispered. *Where did that come from?*

I can't think that way, I have Beth…I'm faithful to Beth.

Beth isn't here now, is she, and you are all alone and human. Just have lunch with her, enjoy yourself. It amazed her that she actually decided to listen to that little voice this time.

Chapter Eight

Jessica's day wasn't getting any better, she was about to go apologize to Luce and ask her if she wanted to grab a bite to eat when she saw her friend and the tall redhead walking out of the office, and in her opinion Luce looked a bit too familiar with the woman. "Jesus, wasn't she just bitching last night about the woman being a bulldog with a bone?" she mumbled. "What happened to 'I don't mess around when I'm with someone…'" *Take it easy, just because she is walking out with the woman doesn't mean she is messing around.*

†

Luce walked back into the office with a smile and whistling a tune. As she approached her desk, Maggie walked toward her with a couple of slips of paper in her hand. "Hey, Luce, I have a couple of messages for you, both from the same person, wouldn't leave a name just a number. Do you want me to run it and see what I can find?"

Her stomach fell, and without really knowing why Luce found herself saying, "No, I'll give a call back, find out myself, but thanks. Anything else I should know about?" she asked, looking at the number, and then back up and flashing Maggie a smile. "Uh, no…" Maggie stuttered, her cheeks turning pink. "I just wanted to make sure you got the messages." Maggie quickly turned on her heel and fled.

"Thank you, Maggie," Luce called as the woman made a hasty retreat to her desk. *Huh. Wonder what that's all about?*

Luce watched the retreating woman for a moment then looked again at the slips of paper in her hand. She didn't recognize the number, and knew she should have had Maggie run it through their databanks and see what came up, but something told her not to. This was something she needed to deal with on her own. Luce turned around and went back the way she came, reaching for her cell phone once she got to her car. As she opened the door and slid in she was already dialing the number on the slips of paper. The moment it was answered and she heard the voice on the other end her heart leaped. "Beth, where are you?" she asked.

"I can't tell you, Luce. I'm not even supposed to be speaking to you but I just couldn't go one more day without hearing your voice," Beth said. "How are you? I heard you went back to work but other than that they won't tell me anything."

"I'm fine, getting stronger every day. How about you, babe? Jessica won't tell me a damned thing about where you are or how you are; all she says is that you're in danger."

"Listen, Luce, I don't have much time to talk, right now. I'm supposed to be at work. But I needed to hear your voice and talk to you, hear that you're all right. I also need you to talk to that agent and prove to her that I'm innocent."

"No, no…Beth…baby, you're being held in protective custody, that's all. Once all this is settled you'll be back with me in my arms. Why do you say you have to prove your innocence, that's ridiculous?" Luce tried to figure out why Beth would say something like that.

"Oh, well, of course she wouldn't have told you that," Beth responded with the sound of annoyance deeply threaded throughout her voice. "Tell me, Luce, has she worked herself back into your bed?" she said, the annoyance turning to outrage.

Instantly Luce's defenses were up as well as her anger. In a tight voice she responded, "Check yourself, Beth, I don't screw around, and Jessica isn't interested in me that way."

With a wicked laugh, Beth replied, "Oh please, Luce, you were lying to me from the first minute you met me, and you kept lying to me. So, honestly, how do I know what you really do or don't do? Either way I need to go, gotta get to work. I'll be in touch with you when I feel it's safe." Then the line went dead. When Luce redialed, her call went straight to voice mail, telling her Beth had turned off the cell phone. Closing her eyes and leaning her head back against the headrest, Luce let out a sigh. She realized Beth had a valid point. She had lied from the moment they met. "Fuck, now what do I do, and just what the hell was that about Jess?" Luce said aloud as she reached for the door handle. With her strides long, it didn't take her long to reach Jessica's office. She knocked and without waiting for an answer opened the door and walked in.

"I want to know what the hell went on between you and Beth while I was in the hospital…and I want to know everything," she said to Jessica, whose look clearly told Luce that she was irritated.

"First off, just what the hell gives you the right to storm into my office? Secondly, what the hell are you talking about," Jessica asked as she stood up from her desk and walked over to the credenza where a pitcher of water sat. Pouring a glass, she waited for Luce to explain.

"I heard from a little bird that you suspect Beth of something other than being a target. Is that true?" Luce asked the anger in her tone barely restrained.

"What little bird would that be? Beth herself? And if I do, what difference does it make, I still need to prove it, don't I? Never mind, you don't have to tell me you've been in contact with her. It really doesn't surprise me that she doesn't know how to follow the rules," Jessica replied as she turned and walked back to her desk.

"God, you're in a bad mood. What's wrong? Didn't that little girl make all your cares go away?" Luce smarted off, not sure why she even went there.

"Luce…do me a favor, stay out of my sex life and I'll stay out of yours," Jessica replied as she turned away and looked out the window of her office.

"What sex life? Do you see me with anyone at the moment? Do you know of anyone other than Beth that I'm interested in?" Luce shot back.

"No, and that's a problem for me. Beth is using you and you're too goddamn horny for the bitch or too stupid to see that."

"What the fuck is your problem? You're behaving like a fucking jealous girlfriend, and we both know you're not that. So spill it."

"And you're not? You're the one making all the damn comments about my sex life and who I choose to spend the night with."

"Ha, don't flatter yourself. I got over you a long time ago," Luce uttered as she turned and walked out of the office. *What the hell just happened,* she asked as she walked to her desk.

Jessica stared at Luce's back as she walked away. Oh, god, those legs just won't quit, and those shoulders look like they've gotten much more muscle on them. *Stop lying to yourself, you know you want her, just do it,* she heard the little voice in her head say. Walking to her door, she kicked it shut with her high-heeled clad foot. "Damn, it I gotta stop thinking that way. Shit, this is the reason I hate coming back here." She walked to her desk and picked up the phone and punched in a number. After an exchange she grabbed her purse and headed out the door.

Chapter Nine

From her desk, Luce watched Jessica walk out of the office. The black heels accentuated her legs, which were wrapped in stockings that left Luce imagining what else she wore underneath the gray business skirt with the slit up the back.

Luce thought back to the first time she saw Jessica. She remembered she had been wearing heels then too, and she remembered the warm feeling she had. She remembered the thrill that went through her when Jessica smiled at her, and to her surprise, she realized she still got that same thrill even now. She got that warm feeling when Jessica spoke to her. A heat raged through her when Jessica innocently touched her as well. Yes, it was all still there.

The thought of her hand on those legs worked like a bucket of cold water hitting her. Whoa, where did that come from? I shouldn't be thinking that way. I am with Beth, and I don't play around on anyone.

Where is Beth? Does she really miss you or does she just want your help to get out of a jam? It's really too bad she doesn't have the same stand-up principles with loyalty. She was with Vargas when she hooked up with you wasn't she? Listening to that voice kept her alive, but that didn't mean that she always liked hearing it. This was one of those times. Unfortunately when she actually took the time to consider what that voice said where Beth was concerned, she realized she had ignored it quite a lot recently. Joe was dead because she didn't listen; she almost died because she ignored that voice, all because she had contacted Beth. She knew it wasn't entirely safe but she saw her anyway. Worst of all Jessica had been placed in danger because of that action. What if Vargas had heard or seen Jessica coming over the slope that day?

"Stop it. Beth isn't the issue. Jessica is going after her for no reason at all. I need to find out why Jessica has her sights set on Beth," she said aloud as she pulled up a screen on her computer. The rest of the afternoon Luce worked on trying to find out more about Beth's past and exactly what she meant when she said Jessica wanted to prove her guilty. She pored through files and through her memory, grasping at anything that could point to guilt on Beth's part. She couldn't come up with anything at all. "Okay, time to look at Vargas and his associates again." She looked at the clock and, seeing that it was after six, decided to call it a day. Vargas and his buddies could wait till tomorrow. She shut down the computer and locked the files she was working on in her desk drawer. She stood, grabbed her jacket, and walked out.

As she walked, the sounds of traffic assaulted her ears and the smell of exhaust penetrated her lungs. God, there were times she really hated the city, but the walk would serve to clear the jumbled thoughts in her head, and God knows she needed that at the moment. She walked down blocks of buildings that held shops, offices, and restaurants. When she realized she was near her favorite diner, she decided that a bite to eat and a good cup of coffee would hit the spot. Walking the half block she turned to her right and entered the doorway. Given the time of evening, the place wasn't packed as it generally was so finding a table wasn't hard at all, and soon May was there with coffee in hand and a menu. "Well, hello there, sweet cheeks," the woman said, flirting with Luce.

"Hey, May, what's good today?" Luce asked with a smile, knowing what the answer would be.

"Well, me for starters, but we can let that go until after dinner. Maybe for dessert you can find out for yourself," the woman replied.

"God, woman, you are such a tease." Luce laughed.

"Only with you darlin', only with you. How are ya, baby? Haven't seen you around in a while, where ya been?"

"Recuperating. It seems a person's body doesn't like being shot," Luce replied, a bit uncomfortable.

"Oh, my god, Luce, I didn't know."

"It's okay, May, I know you didn't. Just wrong place at the wrong time I suppose. So listen, how about some pot roast, mashed potatoes, and green beans," Luce said to change the subject.

"Okay, I get it, you don't want to talk about it. I'll get your order turned in and be back soon with a refill on coffee." Luce watched as the woman walked away, stopping at each table to make sure her customers had everything they needed. Luce rubbed her forehead with her thumb and index finger, knowing the headache she was developing wasn't going to go away anytime soon. Sitting back, she stretched her head to one shoulder then the other before rolling it around in a circle, hoping to loosen the neck muscles. The action did little to relax her.

Letting out a sigh, Luce picked up her coffee cup and took a drink of the hot liquid. The aroma wafting up her nostrils and waking her senses did help give her some control of her mind. As she placed the cup back down she heard the doorbell above the diner's door ring and her eyes looked to the entrance. She smiled when she saw Maggie standing there as if she were looking for someone. When Maggie glanced in her direction, she nodded her head as a greeting and instantly saw Maggie's smile. Before Luce realized what she was doing, she found herself motioning for the other woman to join her. As she watched Maggie approach her table, Luce thought, *what are you doing?*

"Hello, Agent Velazquez, I didn't realize you'd be here."

"It's Luce when we are off duty. I try to come here about once a week. They serve great food," Luce said with a smile. "Care to join me?"

"Oh, I couldn't. I only stopped in to see if my friend was here, and since it doesn't look like he is, I think I'll head on home." Luce found her smile dying and a sense of disappointment settling in as she heard Maggie. "I'm sorry your friend isn't here, but, well, you are and I don't really like eating alone. I'd really like the company. If you want, that is." Luce stopped as she found herself rambling and Maggie's smile growing larger.

"Are you sure? I don't want to disturb you."

"Oh, please." Luce stood up and motioned to the seat in front of her. "Sit down. Would you like some coffee? I'll get May over here… May, can we get another cup of coffee?" she spoke loudly.

With Maggie seated and the coffee on the way, Luce sat back down and flashed Maggie a brilliant smile. "So um, thanks for joining me."

"Thank you for offering. I suppose I should confess I lied when I said I was meeting someone. I got self-conscious when I saw you here," Maggie replied as she looked around the diner.

"You did, uh why?" Luce asked, a little bewildered.

"I…I just didn't expect anyone I know to be here," Maggie replied, hoping her answer would suffice.

"Oh, well, like I said, I come here at least once a week. May's partner and I are friends, so I guess you can say I have a reserved table."

"They do have fantastic food. Oh, thank you," Maggie said to May as she set the coffee down.

"What will it be, sweetie?" the waitress asked as she took out her notepad.

"I think I'll have a side salad, chicken fried steak with potatoes."

"Fantastic choice. Luce, I'll have your dinner shortly or do you want me to bring it at the same time as I bring your friend's?"

"Bring them at the same time please."

"Okay, sweetie, will do," May said then walked away to place the order.

Maggie looked across the table and instantly got nervous. She reached for her glass of water and proceeded to knock it over. "Oh shit," she said as it quickly ran off the edge of the table.

"Whoa," Luce said as she reached for her napkin to help clean it up. Within seconds, May was there with a towel to clean up the mess.

"I'm so sorry," Maggie said, rushing her words together.

"Don't worry about, hon, accidents happen," May replied as she wiped up the last of the liquid. "I'll bring you some more water, okay."

"Thank you."

"Well, that brought some excitement to the table, way to go, Mags…" Luce teased the woman as she flashed a smile and a wink.

"Yes, well, that's me; if I don't cause some kind of commotion then my day isn't complete," Maggie replied as she blushed.

"Hey, accidents happen, right," Luce said as she smiled that smile that shot straight to Maggie's heart.

Maggie couldn't deny it anymore; she was head over heels crazy for Agent Lucinda Velazquez. And the fact that she was sharing a meal with her was far beyond her wildest imagination—well, no, take that back, Maggie had a very imaginative mind. She couldn't say that she had expected

Luce to even notice her, so was shocked when after the first meeting with her the tall agent remembered her name. It made Maggie's heart sing.

†

Amanda had read file after file when she got back to her desk, and here she was reading more at home. She wanted to find whatever she could about Elizabeth Sue Ryan, which wasn't much. Beth was thirty-five-years-old, both parents deceased, one sister who lived forty-five minutes away. Attended CSU, graduated with a master's in business, and ended up working for Judge Marcus Stone. From what she could piece together, months after she started to work for Judge Stone, an affair ensued. It lasted until Vargas entered the picture about two years ago. "Hmm, looks like Ms. Ryan was looking for the bigger, better deal. I wonder what happens now that Vargas is dead." She sat back and stretched, picked up her cell phone, punched in a number, and waited for Ron to answer.

"Hello."

"Hey, Ron, got a question. Are any of the interns there, I need some research done."

"Yeah, Mike will be back soon what do you need?"

"I need to see if Judge Stone and Donavon Vargas ever had dealings. I find it a little coincidental that Ms. Ryan was involved with both. Tell Mike to call me. I'll have some specific instructions on what I'm looking for, okay?"

"Okay, I'll tell him when he gets back. How did your meeting with the ace agent go?"

"Let's just say she is definitely interesting and leave it at that."

"Uh-oh, did she get your interest, Mandy, you devil you…" Ron laughed at the other end of the line.

"Didn't say that. I said she was interesting, besides she says she is involved," Amanda replied as her thoughts went to the dark-haired, blue-eyed woman who charmed her during their impromptu lunch date.

"Okay, so does that mean you've got a story or what?" Ron asked as he sat back in his chair, imagining Amanda on the other end of the line, tapping a pencil, which is what he thought he heard in the background.

†

The car that drove up in the empty parking lot came to a stop and Tyler stepped out. Stuffing his hands into his pockets, he casually walked toward Jessica, who had stepped out of her car. "What's up SAC Sullivan?"

"Sorry to call you out here like this, I'm just not sure who can be trusted in the office. I've been going over files trying to narrow down suspects since I got into town. I know you gave me the lead on this, and I hope I didn't step on any toes when I put Agent Foreman on leave. Please know that I did have very good reason for doing so."

"No trouble at all. As for Foreman, he can be…how do I put it, a tad overbearing maybe."

"That's not the word I was thinking of. I know I mentioned some of why I suspended him. He lost control of the situation and the case that night. Then he suggested it would be better to be above me than under."

"That little bastard," Tyler said.

"I have some questions and right now I think you're the only one that can answer them," Jessica said.

Tyler took his hands out of his pockets and crossed his arms. "Okay, shoot."

"We can sit in the car if you'd like." She motioned to her car, and when Tyler shook his head, she continued. "I want your impression of both Foreman and Cafferty."

"Let's walk," Tyler said as he took a step. "Foreman, as you stated, has been a bit out of control. He wasn't always that way but lately he's lost focus, addled I guess is a good term. Used to be a hell of an agent until about five years ago."

"That's what confuses me. Any idea what happened?"

"None. As for Cafferty, he's a complete arrogant ass. Unfortunately, I can't fire him for that. He is a smart man, well educated, comes from a wealthy family. Can't for the life of me see why he joined the agency? He isn't really a go-getter."

"Ever notice any trouble with his cases being dismissed or evidence gone missing?"

"Can't say that I've really thought about it. Are you seeing something I've missed?"

"Let's go back to the car and I'll show you what I've come up with," Jessica said as she turned and headed back to her car. Tyler followed her and slid into the passenger seat. "I've gone through at least ten case files that both Foreman and Cafferty worked on where the perp walked either due to missing evidence or misplaced files. Somehow they are all tied to Vargas's organization."

"So it looks like we have the leak," Tyler said quietly.

"I don't know although it looks like it. I just can't find the connection between Vargas and the two."

"So what you're saying is that, so far, this is all just speculation. How the hell do we prove anything?" Tyler asked.

Jessica stared out the windshield. "That, sir, is the million-dollar question. Do you recall ever seeing the two acting differently?"

"No. I know they worked assignments together, often butting heads, but not once did I get the impression that they were friends," Tyler answered.

"All right. Well, I've gone through the cases from front to back more than once, along with others that other agents have worked.   And it is only in cases they have worked that suspects walk. We have to figure out why," Jessica said as she turned her gaze toward the man.

"Yeah, again how…" Tyler grumbled in frustration.

"Let's keep our eyes on these two, especially Cafferty. I'll give Foreman a call, have him come in and talk; maybe he'll slip. Look, thanks for meeting me. I know you have a lot on your plate…and I'm sorry I just added more to it."

"Hell, Jess, at the moment we both have a lot on our plates. My top priority is bringing down Vargas's organization. I can't do that if there is someone leaking info. So let's get this wrapped up and hang them all. I'll catch you back at the office," Tyler said as he slid out of the car and walked toward his own vehicle.

"Oh, yeah! Bright and early."

Chapter Ten

Luce had gone home after having a pleasant meal with Maggie. She hadn't really expected to enjoy the company as much as she had, and under different circumstances, the evening would have ended much differently. But tonight she found herself with conflicting feelings. She found herself angry at Beth for not being there with her, and wondered if she was wrong about things. She knew Jessica well enough to know that she didn't just jump at something without a good reason. There was a reason she was suspicious of Beth, and Luce was smart enough to realize it didn't have anything to do with how Jessica felt or didn't feel about her. She was pacing around her living room, glass of scotch in hand, turning thoughts over and over in her head, when she heard a knock on her front door.

Opening the door Luce was surprised when Jessica walked up to her and wrapped her right arm around her neck and kissed her. The kiss was soft, tender, and Luce could taste the whiskey Jessica had been drinking.

Closing the door Luce deepened the kiss as Jessica pulled at Luce's shirt and her fingertips touched the firm muscles of Luce's back. The feel of Jessica's fingers on her skin penetrated Luce's brain and she brought her hands to Jessica's shoulders and pushed her gently away.

"Please don't do that," Jessica said softly.

"Jess, we can't, you know that."

Jessica cleared her throat and stepped back as her hands dropped to her side. She turned away. "I'm sorry, I shouldn't have come here and done that…I need to go."

Luce's hand shot out and grabbed Jessica's arm. "No, you're in no condition to drive. Come on, let's go get some coffee, okay?"

"Luce, you don't…you don't have to take care of me."

"I know I don't, but you're my best friend in this entire world. Do you think I'd just let you leave knowing that you've been drinking?"

"I'm fine, I got myself here, and I can get myself home."

"Yes, and should you have even been behind the wheel? No, you shouldn't have been. So there is no way I can let you get behind it again. Come on, let's get some coffee," Luce said as she tugged Jessica toward the kitchen.

As Luce put the coffee to brew Jessica said, "I'm sorry for what I did back there. I don't know what I was thinking."

"You have nothing to be sorry for, sweetheart," Luce said as she watched Jessica lay her head down on the table. She knew Jess would be out in a matter of seconds. Judging by her breathing, Luce guessed she was already gone. Luce walked over to the woman, gently lifted her up, and then walked to her bedroom. After laying Jessica on the bed, she took off Jessica's silk blouse and then her skirt, before heading back out to the living room. It was a couple of hours later when she finally dragged herself back to her bedroom and climbed into her bed next to Jessica and swiftly fell asleep.

✝

The next morning Luce woke later than normal, stretched her aching body before swinging her legs over the side of the bed. She headed for the kitchen to put some coffee on to brew only to find a freshly brewed pot ready for her, along with a note from Jessica stating she would see her later at the office.

Luce poured a cup of coffee, added sugar and cream to it, then walked with the cup to the bathroom and turned on the shower. She went back to the subject that had occupied her thoughts until at least four in the morning…Beth. Why did Jessica have it out for her? She knew Jessica and knew her well, and not once did she ever remember Jessica's gut feeling being wrong. It was during the long dark hours of the early morning that Luce finally stood back and actually looked at Beth in a clear light. Now under the stream of hot water she faced some cold facts in her relationship with the woman…when push came to shove…she didn't trust Beth.

Jessica stared out the window of her office trying to remember just what the hell she had done. *Exactly what you wanted to happen when you knocked on her door,* the little voice in her head said. "Shit, this is a fucking mess," she said aloud, even as she relived the feel of Luce's fingers on her body and the taste of her skin. God, she missed those lips, the arms that wrapped around her and the feel of Luce's body pressed against hers. All she could think about was the feel of Luce's body moving over hers, and the way Luce had always been able to take her all the way to the moon and stars then back again. Hell, just thinking about it got Jessica wet all over again. The knock on the door brought her back to the present. Letting out a sigh she said, "Yeah," and walked to her desk.

Luce opened the door and strolled in. "Mornin', you were gone when I woke up; you okay?"

"Yeah, why wouldn't I be?" Jessica replied.

"I was just asking, is all. About last night…" Luce said as she sat down in the chair in front of Jessica's desk.

"Yeah, about last night. Look, I know it meant nothing, and I really know it shouldn't have happened and probably wouldn't have if I hadn't stopped by. I'm sorry."

"Jess…nothing happened between us. You had a few too many, fell asleep and I put you in bed…yeah, I undressed you but that was all."

"Really…you did?" Jessica asked, her voice holding a trace of surprise.

"Yeah, really," Luce replied. Her feelings were a little hurt that Jess would think she would take advantage of the situation.

"Oh God, I'm sorry, Luce. I shouldn't have jumped to conclusions."

"Look, Jess, I'm not gonna lie. You and me, we go way back and this…thing… it's like when we're together there's this electricity between us that we can't ignore. I'm well aware that this isn't the time to get into it. But trust me, at some point, we're gonna have to. So you better get used to the idea," Luce said as turned toward the door and left the room.

Jessica followed Luce out the door and said, "Stop and talk to me please." She hurried to catch up with Luce who was ignoring Jessica's plea.

"Damn it, Lucinda Velazquez, stop!" Jessica shouted, not caring who was in the office to hear.

Luce stopped in her tracks, the anger blazing to life in her eyes as she turned. "WHAT do you want from me?" she shouted back.

"I want…I want to know why…" Jessica replied as she lost all fight.

Confused Luce turned and walked back to Jessica, a small frown furrowing her brow. With a sigh she reached for Jessica's arm and led her back toward her office. "Come on, let's talk."

Once in the privacy of the office, Luce asked, "Why what?"

"Why didn't you want to have sex with me last night…why Beth, why…why couldn't we make it work between us?"

"Wait, you're mad at me because I didn't take advantage of you?" Luce asked in confusion as she sank into a chair in front of the desk.

"Yes...no, hell, Luce, I don't know anymore. When I'm around you it's like I can't think straight. Nothing makes sense."

"Jess, let me answer what I can. Why Beth...I don't know. At the time it seemed like a good idea. Let me explain," Luce said as she put her hand up to forestall Jessica who was about to go off. "Beth seemed stable, something I could use as an anchor...I know, stupid idea given the circumstances. When I step back and actually take a good look at things, I was grasping for something that resembled normal. What's more normal than a relationship?"

"Did you...do you love her?" Jessica asked.

"I don't know. I thought I did at the time...now, I honestly can't say. What I can say is with distance there is clarity, and there's something about her that's off. Why I didn't see it before, I don't know."

"Tell me what you see now that you've taken a step back," Jessica said.

"Again, that I don't trust her. I'm not sure why, but I don't. Something is screaming to me that she isn't being honest. I can't tell you what it is that is screaming, and what she has told me that I don't believe now. I know I defended her to you, and swore that I loved her, and how wrong you were about her, but honestly right now, at this moment, I can't say she isn't guilty of something. I just don't know what. I do know that I need to figure this out...and we, you and I, need to figure this," Luce waved her hand in the space between the two of them, "whatever this is, out. Have dinner with me."

"I'm not sure that's a good idea," Jessica said as her right hand went to the back of her neck and massaged the tight muscles.

"It's just dinner. My place at, say, seven o'clock?"

"Dinner…that's all. Besides, I need to float something by you about fellow agents, and I don't feel comfortable talking in the office. But why don't we meet somewhere?"

"I can control myself, sugar, can't you?" Luce replied with that cocky grin that always shot straight to Jessica's heart.

"Always," Jessica said, knowing she was playing with fire and praying neither would be burned. As Luce stood and walked out the door, Jessica shook her head and sat down, mulling over what Luce had said. Sometime later, she pulled a file out of her drawer and started working on her case.

†

She was deep into it when Maggie buzzed in letting her know that James Foreman was asking to see her. "Well, that's an interesting development," she said into the phone. "Give me a minute then send him in please."

She took the minute to close the file and pull out a clean tablet then stood up and walked to open the door. "Mr. Foreman, please come in," she said as she stepped aside. "What can I do for you?" she asked once he was in the office.

"I figured it was about time I came in to talk. I suppose I should apologize for my behavior the night you came into town. There was a lot of shit going down and I was out of line in what I said."

"Mr. Foreman, you were more than out of line, you were treading very close to sexual harassment. Charges that might still be filed, I haven't decided yet. So why don't you tell me why I should let it slide."

"I…look, I was in a bad spot. I'd just found out that we'd lost an agent, and a major crime figure was in custody, emotions were running high. Maybe we can…I don't know…I just can't talk here."

"Mr. Foreman, I really don't know what you want me to do here," Jessica said as she stared at the man.

"I guess coming here was a bad idea. I'm sorry to have taken up your time," James said as he stood up.

Jessica stood and walked around her desk. "Mr. Foreman, I don't understand the reason for this visit. I mean, I really honestly don't believe it was just to apologize."

"Maybe it wasn't, I don't know, but it was clearly a mistake, I'm sorry," he said as he walked to the door and went to open it. Jessica placed her hand on the doorknob and said, "I'm about to head to the coffee shop two blocks down. If you want to talk away from here, then I'll see you there. If not then I suppose you really didn't have anything to say." She then opened the door and let the man out. After a reasonable amount of time, she grabbed her purse and headed out the door on her way to the coffee shop.

Chapter Eleven

Luce walked into the newspaper office and asked to speak with Amanda. Once she was pointed in the right direction, she made her way to the redhead's desk. "Ms. Murphy, how are you doin' today?"

"Well, hello there. I'm doin' well. I never imagined I'd see you here. What can I do for you?"

"I've been thinking, and figured I'd ask a few questions."

"Okay then, why don't you have a seat and ask away," Amanda said as she leaned back in her chair and watched Luce sit down.

"Tell me what you're thinking your angle would be on this story of yours."

"I'm not entirely sure yet. Right now I'm looking for information, doing research," Amanda answered.

"And after the research is done?"

"The story writes itself usually. Have you decided to help?"

"Here's the thing, I'm trying to find info on Beth and the minute I say I'm a fed I either get the door shut in my face or the phone slammed down. I can't find anything out. I'm wondering if you can do better, what do you think?"

"I think there are a lot of questions that need answers; asked correctly I think we can get them."

"Okay, how about a deal. What if we work at this together? I can't seem to get anywhere, like I said, but I need answers. I'm proposing a trade…I help you, you help me. But

I need your word that whatever story you come up with doesn't get printed until I give the okay."

Taking a deep breath Amanda stared at Luce. Letting her breath go she said, "It had better be a damned good story, Velazquez."

"It will be. I guess this is where you start asking me questions, right?" Luce said as she leaned forward in her seat and placed her elbows on her knees.

"Actually, here is where you give me the list of people you need answers from. I'll get started on it, and once I have some answers for you, then I'll get your side of things. How does that sound?"

Luce sat back as she took in what Amanda had just said. "Sounds good to me, but is this a deal you can live with? Is your editor gonna be all right with this?" she asked.

"Stan will deal; he knows I'll come up with a killer story."

"Okay then, we have a deal," Luce replied. "What do you need from me to get started?"

"Just the list of names and a little time to work my magic is all. I'll be in touch when I have something," Amanda said as she stood up to shake hands with her new "partner."

"All right then, I guess I'll head back to work. I'll send the list of names over once I get back to the office."

"Oh, I do have a question for you. Do you know anything about the shootout that left Vargas dead?"

Luce had just reached for the doorknob when the question came. Mentally she bristled and turned to face the redhead. "Why would I know anything about that?"

"I was just curious, especially since you were just released from the hospital for treatment of a gunshot wound. Word is an agent was involved and unless I miss my guess, that agent was you."

"Ya know, red, I'm not sure we're ready for this much info yet."

"That's what I thought," Amanda said as she looked back at her computer screen. "Oh, Agent, don't think I'll forget that question anytime soon."

Luce walked out the door and kept walking, holding her hand up in acknowledgment as she left. She knew at some point she would have to deal with telling the reporter everything that had happened in the last year, ending with the shootout at the park. "I'll just have to deal with that when the time comes," she muttered as she made her way to her vehicle. Opening the car door and sliding in, she put her key into the ignition and drove off, forgetting the reporter and thinking about her dinner plans.

"I need to stop off at the store and pick up some steaks, a couple of lobster tails. Wonder what side dish I can fix, and do I need a salad…and maybe something for dessert," she said as she pulled into traffic. With a smile on her face and humming a tune she headed to the grocery store to pick up dinner.

†

A couple of hours later Luce was unloading the bags of food she had picked up and placing the items in their respective places. It was only when she picked up the bottles of wine did she realize it was Jessica's favorite Mascato, and that she had two bottles. Now that she thought through all the things she bought, she realized she had picked up pretty much all Jessica's favorites, right down to the death by chocolate cake. "I just want her to enjoy dinner is all," she said as she put the two bottles of wine in the refrigerator. Luce walked to the living room and glanced at the pile of folders sitting on the coffee table. She considered working but decided to go for a run instead. The folders would be there later anyway. She went to her bedroom and changed into her running clothes and headed out the back door.

†

Jessica had returned to the office for a few hours after her coffee break. She had waited for a good forty-five minutes for Foreman to show up before she realized that he wasn't going to. Well, it was worth a shot, she thought. He said he had something he wanted to talk about, but didn't want to say anything at the office, and yet he knew where she would be and didn't bother to stop by. "What's on your mind, Mr. Foreman?" she said as she tapped her pen on the desk. With a sigh, she rolled her shoulders, reached for her purse, stood, and headed out the door. She wasn't getting any work done so she decided she would head home, take a nice hot bath, and maybe get the brain going again. Then she would be clearheaded for dinner with Luce, and could talk things over with her.

At home, she opened the door and dropped her keys on the table that sat just inside doorway and headed to the kitchen in search of something to drink. She heard Tom shout, "Hey, Jess, grab me a beer would ya?"

"Sure, you want me to make you a sandwich too?" she shouted back sarcastically.

"Well, only if you want to."

With a shake of her head she went to the fridge, grabbed two bottles of beer and opened them. Heading in the direction of her brother's voice, she found him in the office.

"Here you go," she said as she handed Tom his beer.

"Hey, sis, where were you last night?" he asked as he sat back, looking at Jessica as he took a long drink from the bottle.

"Out," Jessica replied as she took a sip. "How was your evening?"

"I'm gonna say probably not as interesting as yours. I stayed in, watched some TV and slept in my own comfy bed," Tom answered.

"I don't know whether to be happy or sad for you," Jessica said, laughing.

"It wasn't so bad actually. Maybe you should try it." Tom laughed as well. "What's the plan for tonight, sis?"

"I have some things I need to talk over with Luce. Hopefully get both my case and my life straightened out," Jessica said as she thought about the night before. *What the hell am I doing?* she wondered for what seemed like the hundredth time. Sitting up straighter in his chair Tom said, "Okay, time for some talk time, what's goin' on with you and her?"

"In a nutshell…I don't know. Lately, I find myself wondering if I made a mistake letting her go all those years ago. I miss everything about her, and no one, and I do mean no one, makes me forget her."

"So you're sayin' you're still hung up on her."

"NO, I mean, maybe…yes. Why shouldn't I be? She is fun to be around, intelligent, hardworking, honorable…amazing eyes, she is gentle, loving, caring…"

"All right and what, she wasn't all these things before?"

"She was. It was just…I don't know I suppose it was being young and not willing to make things work. It was too easy to just let things end I suppose."

"Okay and now? It's not like you can just pop back into her life and pick up where you left off, right?"

"How the hell do I know?" Jessica shot back. "I mean, it's not like I can just blurt out 'hey I want another chance,' now can I?"

"Why not? Unless she is already in a relationship, she might be receptive," Tom said as he lifted the bottle to take another drink.

"I don't know, maybe too much water under the bridge," Jessica replied as she stood up. "I'm gonna grab a shower, maybe try to relax a little before I head over to her place."

"All right, I won't wait up for you then." Tom laughed as he sat forward to once again concentrate on the papers in front of him.

Chapter Twelve

Luce had just finished mixing the salad when she heard a knock on the door. Wiping her hands on a towel, she walked through the living room, to let Jessica in. "Hey there," she said as she opened the door. "Come on in, let me take your purse. I just got the salad together and was waiting for you to throw the steaks on the grill. You look fantastic, by the way," she said as she led Jessica to the backyard. "Would you like something to drink?"

"Uh, no thanks, I think I'm good for now. Wow, I'd forgotten how beautiful it is out here," Jessica said as she stepped out onto the deck. The yard had two parts to it—the cooking and dining area, and a pool area. Potted plants were arranged throughout the space, which provided a relaxing and inviting place. Lounge chairs were arranged around the pool area along with small tables for drinks, again it was an inviting place meant for relaxation and fun.

"It's been a while since you've been out here. Course that would probably be because it's been a while since you've been in town."

"God, Luce, are we going to go through this again?" Jessica asked, a trace of frustration edging into her voice.

"Nah, was just sayin' is all. Come on, Jessie, relax, kick off your shoes, sit down, have a drink and enjoy, all right."

"You know, I think maybe this was a bad idea," Jessica said as she as she turned to go back through the door she had just come through.

"Jess…sit down and relax. I didn't mean anything by that other than I've missed you and would like to see you more. That's all I was saying," Luce said as she took a step toward her longtime friend.

With a sigh Jessica replied, "Sorry, I guess I'm a little touchy about things."

"Ya think? Look, let it go. You had a damn good job offer and you had to take it. I understand. Hell, I probably would have made the same call, and for the record I'm not Gloria."

"No, you aren't. I'm sorry. Maybe I feel guiltier about things than I want to."

"Jess, it's in the past. Are you happy doing what you're doing?"

"Yeah," Jessica replied.

"Then that's all that matters. Last I heard Gloria is extremely happy with her life, you appear to be happy with your choices, so why are you so touchy?"

"I guess I'm second-guessing my choices. Or maybe I'm not all that happy with the choices," Jessica said, walking to the mini fridge she knew held beer. She opened it and withdrew a bottle, twisted off the cap and took a long drink before sitting in a chair.

"So talk to me," Luce said as she turned to face Jessica after throwing the two thick T-bones on the hot grill.

"I'm almost thirty-six and all I have is my damned job. I have no one to come home to at night, an apartment I see maybe three times a week, and friends I have no idea if I'll ever see again when they leave the office on an assignment. I guess I'm wondering how different my life would have been if I'd made different choices. Do you ever feel that way, Luce?" Jessica sat forward and leaned on her elbows as she waited for an answer.

"Sometimes, yeah, I mean our job makes it kind of hard to have any kind of relationship. It's hard to explain vanishing for days at a time, ya know."

"It's no easier leaving for an investigation, and you certainly don't make friends when agents know you're looking into their lives."

"Trust…it all boils down to trust. Our training and suspicious minds make it damned near impossible to do that, right?"

"For sure," Jessica said as she watched Luce flip the steaks. The aroma of them was making her mouth water. "Anything I can help with?"

"Nope, you still like your steak rare?" Luce asked.

"Of course, is there any other way to eat a steak?"

"Hell no," Luce replied with a chuckle. "Almost ready, babe. Hey, did you bring your swimsuit? I was thinking we could take a swim after dinner."

"No, I didn't even think about it."

"No worries, I probably have one that will fit you," Luce replied. She reached for the plates to put the steaks and a beautifully grilled lobster tail on then carried each plate to the table. She went back to get the grilled yellow and green squash, and placed them on the table as well. "I'll be right back with the salad, need anything else?" she asked from the doorway.

"No everything smells fantastic, I can't wait to dig in to it," Jessica said as she went to the fridge and grabbed one more bottle of beer and one nonalcoholic. She had just placed them in front of each plate when Luce returned with the bowl of salad and two bottles of dressing, one blue cheese and the other red wine vinaigrette.

"Here we go, let's dig in!" Luce said with a smile. "Thanks for the fake beer," she added as she pulled out the chair for Jessica.

"Not at all. Thank you for inviting me over."

"It's good to have you around, my old friend," Luce said as she took her seat, picked up her bottle and took a drink. "Help yourself," she said as she began to cut into her steak, and then her lobster.

After putting some perfectly grilled squash on her plate, Jessica picked up her knife and fork. She closed her eyes the moment the tender steak touched her tongue; she had forgotten how tasty Luce's steaks were. Try as she might she could never figure out the secret marinade Luce had come up with. All she knew was that the steaks had the perfect flavor and were always so tender. "God, I'd forgotten how good your steaks always were," she said as soon as she swallowed her first bite. "Why won't you tell me what your secret is?"

Luce laughed. "Because then you'll know how to make it, never have dinner with me again, and sell the recipe and make millions. Sorry, it's something I can't risk, babe."

"Oh, so it's all about you, I see." Jessica laughed.

"Never give up the opportunity to have dinner with a beautiful woman, is my motto," Luce said as she brought her fork up to her mouth.

"I'd also forgotten how smooth you can be." Jessica smiled as she cut into the vegetables.

"It's coming across like you believe that's a line," Luce said as she held the beer bottle midway to her mouth and looked directly at Jessica.

Jessica looked up as well. "Isn't it? Luce, I know you, know you too well."

"Then you should know I've never used a line on you," Luce said quietly.

"Luce…I know you haven't."

Luce took a drink of her beer, her eyes still holding Jessica's gaze. "So tell me what's going on that you don't want to discuss it at the office."

"I've been looking through case files, looking for leads on dirty agents and came up with some possibilities. I want your thoughts on things."

"Okay, tell me."

"Lots of missing papers and evidence on arrests of people involved in Vargas's organization leading to cases being dismissed and charges dropped; most of the busts were made by either Foreman or Cafferty. Interestingly enough, Foreman paid me a visit this morning; behaved like he wanted to say something but was afraid to. I gave him a chance to meet me away from the prying eyes and ears but he didn't show. I'm curious to know your take on the situation and the players."

"You're saying one or both of them could be responsible for Joe's death?" Luce asked in a cold tone.

"It's looking that way, yes."

Taking a deep breath Luce closed her eyes then let it out slowly as she fought to keep her anger in check. There was nothing she wanted more than to find the two men and put a bullet in each of their heads. She tried to forget the look of fear, the pleading she saw in Joe's eyes seconds before the gun fired. Unwanted images of Rebecca from the night she told her about Joe's death and Joey saluting his father's casket assaulted her and tore at her.

"Luce, baby, are you all right?" Jessica asked as she watched the pained expressions flash over Luce's face.

"Yeah, just…nothing I do will make it right for Rebecca and Joey. I can't…goddamn it, I should have been able to do something."

Jessica stood and went to the side of Luce's chair. Kneeling down she took Luce's hand and said, "Baby, you know there was nothing you could do. There was no way in this world that you could have stopped Marco from pulling the trigger or Vargas from giving the order."

"I didn't even try, Jessie, that's what kills me."

"Did you have time?" Jessica asked. She had read the reports, knew what it was like in situations like that, and knew that Luce didn't.

"We walked into the farmhouse and I saw Joe, all bloody, tied to the chair; fear in his eyes as he looked at me. We both pleaded with Vargas to listen to reason but he wouldn't. Marco was standing there with the gun pointed at Joe, then Vargas gave the order and Marco pulled the trigger," Luce said as she relived the final seconds of her friend's life. "No, there wasn't time."

"Then tell me, sweetheart, what in God's name do you think you could have done?"

"I don't know, but I shouldn't have just stood there and watched my friend die," Luce said as she choked back the tears and pain.

Jessica's heart broke at seeing and hearing the pain coming from Luce. At the moment all she could do was hold her hand and offer her shoulder, which made her feel completely inadequate.

Luce's tears rolled down her face and dropped onto her hand which was clasped in Jessica's. Clearing her throat and pulling herself together as best she could, Luce said, "How certain are you that Foreman and Cafferty are involved in all of this?"

"Like I said, I have dozens of cases that ended up dead in the water due to lost evidence, incorrect information, missing files…way too many for it to be a coincidence, just no evidence," Jessica replied.

"So we need to build an airtight case against them."

"Yeah, that's where I'm at," Jessica said as she stood up and walked toward the minibar. She reached for two rocks glasses, placed ice in each and poured some scotch in them. She walked back to the table and placed one in front of Luce.

"What exactly did Foreman have to say when he visited you?"

With a sigh Jessica said, "He said he came by to apologize for our first meeting the night Joe died. He was acting really strange, though. I got a feeling he wanted to say something but was afraid to. Said he couldn't talk there, so I gave him an option of meeting me elsewhere and he never showed. Luce, he acted like he was afraid of something."

"Foreman is a spineless weasel. I don't see him being the mastermind in this. Cafferty, on the other hand, is a slimy bastard, capable of anything. He slinks around and sticks his nose into everything. It's my bet the asshole has something on Foreman. It's the only thing that makes sense to me. Have you looked into that?"

"Tyler and I are looking into that aspect. I spoke to him before I left for the day. We're going to start looking into Foreman and hopefully we will find out what or even *if* Cafferty is holding something over his head."

"It's a start I suppose," Luce said as she reached out and took the glass of scotch in her hand.

"Luce, you know these people, I don't. Do you believe I'm on the right track? My gut tells me I am, but I need to know what you think."

"Jessie, you know you're seldom wrong. That's why you hold the position you do, trust your gut."

"So you think I'm on to something?"

"Yeah, I do. What do we do to bring Joe's killers down?"

"Luce, I don't know that I can have you involved in this officially."

"What the fuck do you mean? I'm already involved, I know all the players."

"Yes, you do, and you are involved, but not in a helpful way. When this goes to trial, the defense will say you were too close and your judgment was biased, that you may have planted evidence."

"That's bullshit, I'd never plant evidence you know that…" Luce all but shouted at Jessica.

"Don't…I know you would never plant evidence. I also know that you slept with a suspect's woman while undercover. That alone could jeopardize the case. In fact, there could be some people who say had that not happened Joe could still be alive. And before you say anything, I am not one of those people."

"Jesus Christ, do you…I'm not responsible for that. Joe and I were careful. We never spoke in the same place more than once, always made sure we weren't tailed. Hell, we would backtrack four or five times just to make sure. And there is the little fact that I'd be lying alongside Joe if we'd been made."

"Which all points to someone inside feeding information to Vargas. We need to figure out who that is. Tell me what you know or think about both Foreman and Cafferty that can help me."

"Foreman, like I said, is an idiot." Luce looked up from her glass and saw Jessica shaking her head. "What?" she asked.

"Reading his file shows a completely different man than we see today. When he first started, he showed a lot of promise as a leader. Think about it, he had to have some intelligence to get to Agent in Charge, some ambition. Up until about six years ago, Foreman's record showed a strong sense of fair and legal judgment. He followed the law to the letter. Then something happened to change all that. His investigations started to get messy, follow-up was sloppy…appears to me he lost his reason for being a good agent," Jessica stated.

"Money?" Luce asked.

"I don't know. Until we look over his financials tomorrow we won't know. You've known him a while, has he dressed differently, drive a nicer car?"

"No, not that I know of," Luce responded.

"Cafferty, on the other hand, does have a taste for finer clothes and drives a damn nice car," Jessica said as she brought her glass to her lips.

"Maybe he just made good investments, or comes from money," Luce said.

"Luce, I've made good investments, received a very nice inheritance and you don't see me driving around in a car like his. I don't know, there's just something about him that I don't trust. Honestly, he makes my skin crawl."

"Doesn't mean he's dirty, Jessie," Luce said with a sigh. "Look, I can't stand the prick but unless we have something concrete we can't do anything. So I suggest you put into motion the wheels of justice and find a way to make those charges and make sure they stick." Luce stood up and walked to the minibar and grabbed the bottle of scotch. As she poured the amber liquid into Jessica's glass her hand shook with the emotion of buried pain and anger that bubbled just below the surface of her being.

Jessica stood up from her chair. With one hand she covered Luce's, and with the other she took the bottle. She wrapped her arms around the tall woman and whispered into her ear, "Luce, let it go, you don't have to keep it buried, sweetheart. I can't know the pain you're feeling, baby, but you gotta let it go."

With a catch in her voice Luce replied, "I feel like I'll never stop crying if I let go. Jessie, you didn't see the look in Joe's eyes when I walked into that goddamned room. He knew what was coming and I could see him pleading with me to do something," Luce said as the tears slid down her cheeks. "God, both Vargas and Marco were so cold, so...I don't know...eager maybe, to shoot Joe. Vargas kept saying he needed to make an example of Joe."

"Well, he didn't make it to the top by being soft. Of course he had to make an example. He'd just found out Joe infiltrated his organization and he needed to know everyone else understood the consequences of that."

"It was more…now that I think of it, he kept looking at Beth and I, like he suspected something but couldn't prove it. Then he sent Beth away."

"Jesus, Luce, you're damned lucky you weren't put into the same damned hole Joe was. What is it about that woman that blinds you?" Jessica asked with frustration in her voice. She dropped her arms from around Luce and walked back to her chair.

"Jess, it's complicated," Luce said as she sat down.

"Oh, bullshit, be fucking honest with me."

"What do you want me to say…I don't know anything other than I don't trust her completely anymore. I don't know what happened to change that let alone when. Jesus, it was so easy to trust her when we met. I know, of all the people to trust, she's the one I pick."

"No shit, what an idiot move," Jessica said.

"Yeah, I know. Jess, you know my cover when I joined Vargas's organization. I spent the first four months driving Beth around, watching her shop for dresses and shoes and purses. She didn't attend meetings with Vargas, she didn't meet with any of his men, and I'm telling you she doesn't know anything. Even when Vargas started trusting me and including me I never saw anything to even suggest she was involved in anything," Luce said as she stared at the liquid in the glass in her hand.

"I just found myself looking forward to the times I knew I was to accompany her on her shopping trips. I started to feel alive when I was with her and lost when I wasn't. You and I both know that feeling. Jess, I didn't set out to fall for anyone, it just sort happened. Tell me why you don't like her, what is it that makes you go off like you do when her name is mentioned."

With a sigh, Jessica looked at her friend and said, "She's a user. My gut tells me she knows more about Vargas and his dealings than she is telling. I don't like that she is a danger to you as long as you are involved with her, and I really hate that you're blind to her behavior and the danger you're in."

"Okay, fresh eyes then…tell me everything that you see."

"All right, if you're sure you want to hear what I have to say…are you?" Jessica asked as she leaned back into her chair.

"Yeah, I am," Luce replied.

"I'm gonna assume that you read her jacket before you went into this assignment, but let me refresh your memory anyway. Elizabeth Sue Ryan, thirty-five years of age. Elizabeth was a graduate of Colorado State University, with a degree in business. From what we have been able to find, she liked living extravagantly while barely making ends meet, until she landed a job with Judge Marcus Stone. Her living expenses took a drastic jump and rumors started flying about her involvement with the judge. In a strange twist of fate, it turns out that Judge Stone was the presiding judge on more than a few cases involving Vargas and his lower level 'employees.' Then the judge is killed in a home invasion and, boom, Beth is now being seen escorted around town on the arm of none other than Donavon Vargas. Then shortly thereafter you are in the picture."

"Okay, so she likes the expensive things in life, doesn't make her a criminal," Luce said as she stood and began pacing.

"You're right, it doesn't. What it does do is give one a sense of the type of person she is. Having met her and spoken to her, I can tell you she is definitely someone used to getting what she wants, and she doesn't care how she gets it."

"No…that's your bias talking, you don't like her so you're looking for things to fit your profile."

"I wish it were. Luce, before she was taken into protective custody she tried everything she could think of to convince me to let her leave, including coming on to me."

With a disbelieving chuckle Luce said, "No, you misunderstood her actions. Beth doesn't think that way. She isn't conniving or manipulative. She wouldn't have done anything like that."

"You asked me what I saw, I'm telling you. Have you ever had someone you're questioning come on to you…you know, the flirty touches that try to create that personal bond? Beth tried that along with a 'nice shoulder rub,' because, you know, 'I was so tense.' That's a come-on, Luce, and you know it."

"All right, then why go for me? What could I do for her that Vargas couldn't?"

"She enjoys a challenge, playing with fire. The cover you were set up with involved a high price tag—many exotic locations with homes that you 'own' along with an extremely healthy bank account. Maybe she decided you had more to offer and she didn't have to worry about you putting a bullet in her head if she made a wrong step. Sounds plausible to me," Jessica replied. She carefully watched the emotions on her friend's face before she said, "You asked what I saw, I'm telling you, and where I'm coming from. Tell me what happened that you no longer trust her but are still so willing to defend her?"

"As you know, I got a call from her, and no she didn't tell me where she was. She was more focused on me 'proving her innocence' than anything else…well, that and whether you were back in my bed or not," Luce said as she sat back down. "When I said she should know me better than that, she tossed at me how I'd been lying to her since the day we met and that she really doesn't know me, then hung up. When I tried to call her back her phone was off. And before you ask, she hasn't called again," Luce said as she looked at Jessica.

"Do you still have the number she called you from?" Jessica asked.

"Yeah, it's on my cell. I've tried a couple of times to call it and it's still off. I'm thinking she is smart enough have bought a burner. We won't be able to track it."

"Probably not, but it would still be a good idea to try, you know keep an eye on it, see what happens. Luce, would you tell me if she were to call you again?" Jessica asked as she looked straight into Luce's eyes.

"Yeah, of course I would, why would you even ask that?"

"Because I don't know where you stand where she is concerned."

"I suppose I see where you're coming from," Luce replied as she sought answers deep within her. "Joe died because someone gave him up and I need to know who that was. If Beth has answers, then I need to figure out how to get them from her. Jess, I don't know who to trust other than you. Those are the reasons I'll let you know the minute I hear from her again."

"All right, so how do you plan on getting answers from her; especially if she isn't in contact with you?"

"Well, I had a meeting with Amanda Murphy earlier. She is willing to do some footwork in exchange for an exclusive."

"Nice, but are you sure about giving her a story?"

"Hell no, but do I have a choice? The minute anyone hears I'm a fed, they shut me down."

"So what happens if she finds something on Beth you don't want to hear?"

"Shit if I know. Right now, all I know is that I'm tired of thinking. What do you say about a swim?" Luce asked as she rubbed the bridge of her nose and then looked at Jessica.

"Maybe. Let me help you clean up first, then I'll think about it," Jessica said as she smiled at her friend.

Together the two soon had dishes cleared and in the dishwasher, and the leftover veggies in the fridge. Luce had gotten a swimsuit for Jessica and had gone into her room to change as well. Then with two large towels in hand she padded back through the living room just in time to see Jessica walking toward the pool through the large sliding glass doors. She stopped dead in her tracks as a bolt of desire struck straight at her core. It took every ounce of strength she could muster to force herself to start walking again.

"Shit, maybe this wasn't such a good idea," she muttered under her breath as she walked through the same doors to the pool and Jessica.

Chapter Thirteen

Shortly after Jessica left Tom sat back in his chair, his gaze taking in his surroundings. The room was tastefully decorated, as was the rest of the house, with various objects he had collected during his frequent travels. He closed his eyes and enjoyed the softness of his chair and the rich smoky aroma of the cigar that burned in the ashtray on his desk. His risks had paid off well, he thought. With a chuckle, he thought about the way his life had turned out. Not a person in his life ever believed he could be in the position he was in. Not that anyone had ever spoken it, but he knew…he felt it in their looks and heard the murmurs behind his back. Hell, even his own sister had her doubts about him. To be honest, that hurt him a little. He opened his eyes and reached for the glass of scotch. God, he couldn't wait to be finished with his work here so he could head back to his real home in Belize. Hell, for that matter he could go to the villa in the south of France and be perfectly happy. He truly laughed aloud when it occurred to him that no one, not even his sister, realized that this place was nothing…in fact, it was what he considered his shack of a home, when in others' eyes it was high-end. Tom took one last swallow from the glass and walked out of the office toward the kitchen where he dropped off the glass and pulled the cell phone from his pocket. "Meet me in thirty at the warehouse. I want this transaction over with," he said as he walked to his bedroom. *God, Jessica would so totally lecture me…hell, she would probably arrest me if she knew what I was doing here.* It wasn't his fault he was creative and found ways to get merchandise to people. They paid him damned good money for his creativity.

✝

James Foreman pulled into his driveway glad the day was over. He opened the car door and stepped out, rolling his shoulders as he came to his full height. He couldn't wait to kick off his shoes and to have a whiskey and soda in his hand as he relaxed in his recliner. He opened the front door and walked in. As he placed his keys on the small table in the foyer he called out for his wife. "Hey, Mon, I'm home. What's for dinner, I'm starved." He walked into the living room thumbing through the mail as he went.

"Hi, honey," Monica Foreman said as she walked up to him and placed a kiss on his cheek. "Look who stopped in to see us," she said as she walked behind the bar to fix James's drink.

"Hey there, James, how's it going?" Mason said as he stood from where he was seated at the sofa.

"Mason. This is a nice surprise, what brings you by?" Foreman said, hoping his wife couldn't detect the uneasiness in his voice and see the complete panic he was sure was in his eyes.

"Oh, I was just in the neighborhood and thought I'd stop in see how you and your lovely wife are doing."

"I see. Well, we're doing just fine, as you can see. I hope we aren't keeping you from anything, though. Had I known you were stopping by I would have been home sooner," Foreman said as he accepted the drink from his wife.

"Nah, not to worry. Monica and I have been having a nice chat, isn't that right, Monica?" Cafferty said with what he considered his charming smile.

"Of course, we've been having a very nice conversation. Now you two sit down and talk while I go check on dinner, it shouldn't be much longer." Monica said as she started to walk toward the kitchen. Halfway there she stopped and turned. "Mason, why don't you join us? I made plenty and it's been so nice catching up with you that I don't want it to end," she said.

"Oh, Mon, I'm sure Mason has plans. He shouldn't have to change them just to have dinner with us," James said.

"Actually, I'd love to join you. Whatever you're cooking smells delicious and I can promise it would be a hundred times better than the TV dinner I have waiting for me at home," Cafferty said, much to Foreman's dismay.

"Great! I'll put another plate on the dining room table," Monica said with a smile as she went to the kitchen.

"James, you need to relax, you're about to jump out of your skin," Cafferty said, all the while enjoying the effect his presence was having on the other man.

"What the hell are you doing here?" Foreman growled in a low voice.

"Now, now is that anyway to speak to a guest?" Cafferty replied with amusement. "Why don't you show me your backyard? Monica has been telling me that you have some lovely roses, and we really don't want Monica hearing what we are talking about, now do we? Although considering the gift I brought, she may not be in the state to care about much of anything right about now."

"You bastard…she's been clean why would you do that to her?"

"Outside Foreman," Cafferty said as he started to walk to the sliding patio doors.

Though he wanted to run to check on his wife, Foreman had no choice but to follow the man.

"Nice garden you have here. These roses are beautiful. What's your secret to growing them so that they have such vibrant color to them?" Cafferty asked casually. "I once heard about some guy down south dusting them with human ashes;

said he even mixed the ashes into the soil. Kind of creepy if you ask me, but the story is he had prize-winning roses for years. You ain't doing things like that to help these grow are you, Foreman?" Cafferty asked as he snapped a rose off the bush and brought it to his nose to smell it.

"What the hell are you talking about, Cafferty? Tell me why you're here or let's go back in. I want to check on Monica."

With an evil laugh Cafferty said, "Oh relax, you know damn well I don't make deliveries. If she is high, she already had the stuff. I'm more interested in you getting the message."

"And what message is that, Cafferty?" Foreman asked as the little bit of relief he felt for a few seconds was quickly replaced with a cold sweat.

"The message is that you better get your ass in gear and find that bitch Ryan and find out who the Chameleon is. I've given you plenty of time. I want answers by this time tomorrow, you hear me? I'm fucking tired of waiting and losing money because this prick swoops in and takes control of things, because he wants to make sure that bitch isn't gonna turn around and sink everything."

"I'm trying! Jesus, you think it's easy trying to find out shit when no one wants to talk?"

"Do I look like I give a fuck?" Cafferty said as he stepped within an inch of Foreman's face, his eyes cold and menacing. "Tomorrow by this time; now let's put on our smiles, go inside, and eat that delicious dinner your wife made," he said as he stepped back and turned toward the house.

Hours later, Foreman was still roaming around his house trying to find a way out of this mess. It was close to midnight when his cell phone vibrated on the nightstand beside his bed. Quietly he said, "Yeah," and slipped out of the bed carefully so as to not wake his wife. James listened to what the caller had to say then hung up. He spent the next few hours pacing the floor of his office and drinking straight whiskey.

†

Jessica rolled over to answer her phone, which was rattling on the nightstand. Her foggy mind barely registered the red digits of the clock, which read five a.m. "Hello," she said groggily into the phone. "Yeah, this is Jessica Sullivan."

"Uh-huh," she said as stifled a yawn and reached to turn on the bedside lamp. "And I can trust you to actually be there? Yeah, all right, I'll see what I can do. Okay, I'll be there, just make sure you're there," she finished and the hit the end button. Jessica tapped the open phone on her chin as she thought, and then quickly dialed Luce's number.

"Hello?" Luce's sleepy voice came over the line.

"Guess who I just heard from…James Foreman. He wants to talk."

"Oh, yeah? When? Are you meeting him at the office?"

"No, someplace called the Southside Diner," Jessica replied.

"What time do we meet him?" Luce asked.

"We don't. I meet him around four."

"No…no, you don't. I'm going with you."

"You can't. We can't risk him getting spooked."

"Why would he be spooked? Look, he knows I was part of the operation that brought Vargas down. He knows I'm a key player. He wouldn't think anything of me being there," Luce said.

"Yes, but if he is guilty of what we think, he could have someone from the organization watching."

"Yeah, which is why I think you going alone is a bad idea. It could be a trap or something," Luce replied.

"I'm not going alone, he asked for Tyler to be there too."

"Oh great, so the two of you will be targets," Luce said in frustration. She rolled out of bed and reached for the robe that was at the foot of the bed.

"This is why we will never work," Jessica muttered under her breath.

"What?" Luce asked.

"Nothing. I understand what you're saying, okay, but this could very well be the break we need to finally bury Vargas's organization," Jessica argued as she got out of her bed and padded to the kitchen to start some coffee.

"You don't know that this isn't a setup to find out what you know. If Foreman is involved with the organization, he has some very dangerous individuals on his side. People that won't hesitate to shoot first if they feel threatened."

"What, and I don't know that? Seriously, do you take me for an idiot? Luce, I know you aren't happy, but someone needs to meet with Foreman and find out what he knows. He reached out to me that means there is some sort of trust involved, and I can't just ignore that."

"Fine, but all I'm saying is you can't go in there without some cover, or knowing exactly what you're walking in to. Now let's figure this out, 'cause it's gonna be a long-ass day," Luce said as she too walked to her kitchen for coffee.

†

When Jessica finally walked into the office and headed straight to Tyler's door, she already felt as if she had put in a twelve-hour day.

Tapping on the open door, Jessica said, "Hey, got a minute?"

"Yeah, come on in. What's going on?" Tyler said as he sat back in his chair.

"I got an interesting phone call early this morning," Jessica said as she took a seat in front of the big desk. "Something is going on and it has Foreman itchy."

"Oh, yeah? Do tell."

"He wants to meet with you and I later today at a place called the Southside Diner."

"Interesting choice…it's not a place known for being overly friendly and they mind their own business. So what's your plan?" Tyler asked, sitting forward.

"Well, I think we should be there early and make sure our backs are covered. Luce was mad as hell when I told her I was meeting him."

"Jesus, Velazquez doesn't have to be a part of every goddamn thing that goes on," Tyler said with a grin.

"Good luck convincing her of that."

"So how long have you known her?" Tyler asked.

"Long enough," Jessica replied as she squirmed in the seat. She didn't want to get into her relationship with Luce. "Should I meet you there or do you want to ride together?"

"No, I'll meet you there. I want to have a look around, make sure we aren't walking into any surprises. It might be useful to have an exit strategy."

"Yeah, good point. I don't think we'll need it but better to have one than not and be sorry. I'll see you around four then," Jessica said as she walked out, heading to her office.

†

Luce's morning had been long but productive. She had walked the entire block where the diner was located, the blocks on both sides of the street and the one across the street from it. She knew every nook and cranny of the alleyways, located any possible area someone could hide, and knew where every doorway and open window were located.

With a little luck, she would have time to stop off at the office and give Tyler and Jessica a highlight of her findings and some areas that concerned her, before she had to head home and put on her 'work clothes.'

116

†

Jessica pulled her car into a parking spot a building away from the entrance of the diner, and had barely put her car into park when out of nowhere a shabbily dressed person appeared and quickly began spraying her windshield with blue liquid.

"Hey, no, don't do that," she hollered, opening the door and simultaneously turning off the ignition.

"I really don't need my window washed," she said as she jumped out and closed the door. She stepped up to the person and dug into her purse, looking for her billfold. She couldn't just walk away and not give the guy a dollar she thought as she pulled a loose dollar bill out.

"You really haven't learned a damn thing have you?" the woman in ragged dress said as she wiped the windshield.

Jessica frowned as she looked up at the vagrant. "Luce?" she said.

"Yeah, and if you keep looking at me you're gonna blow my cover. How many times have I told you that you can't just hand homeless people money? I could have grabbed your wallet and ran just now. You have to pay attention. You of all people should know that. Jesus!"

"What the hell are you doing here?" Jessica asked in a hushed voice.

"I don't trust Foreman, so I'm here to make sure you're safe. Isn't that obvious? Now just go into the diner before people start to look. Tyler is already in there," Luce said as she held her hand out and took the dollar bill Jessica had brought out of her purse. "Thank you, ma'am, may God bless," Luce said loudly as she walked away, pretending to be in search of another windshield to wash.

Jessica watched Luce walk down the street and disappear into an alley. She actually felt better knowing that Luce was watching out for her.

†

Tyler stood and pulled out a chair when he saw Jessica walking toward him. He had been in the place for at least thirty minutes, watching as the occasional patron came in and left. So far, he saw nothing or anyone that worried him, and he felt comfortable in saying that the meeting Foreman asked for was legit.

"Hey, Jessica," he said as she walked up to the table.

"How's it look, Doug?" she asked.

"Everything looks to be on the up and up. I'll take a trip to the little boys' room here in a few and check out the back just to make sure we don't have any surprises. Foreman should be here anytime, right?"

"Yeah, and just as an FYI we have some backup as well."

"Please don't tell me," Tyler said and moaned as Jessica nodded. "Are you freakin' kiddin' me?"

"Not even. Trust me, though, no one will know it's her. Hell, I didn't even realize it until she spoke to me."

"Well, there's nothing I can do about it right now so I suppose it's better to have her watching our backs," Tyler said as Jessica sat down.

"That's how I'm thinking," Jessica said. "Hi, could I have a glass of iced tea with lemon, please," she asked the waitress who had just stopped at their table.

"Sure thing, sugar. How about you, ya need a refill, honey?" the gray-haired woman asked Tyler.

"Yup, it's the best damn coffee I've had all day!" Tyler winked as he pushed the cup closer to the edge of the table.

With a smile, the waitress poured the coffee and said she would be right back with a glass of iced tea for Jessica. As soon as she walked away, Tyler said he was going to do a walk around through the back and make sure everything was still on the up and up. He had just gotten back and sat down when the door opened and James Foreman walked in. He headed straight toward the table and pulled out a chair. They were exchanging pleasantries when the waitress appeared with Jessica's tea and a coffeepot. Once she had poured a cup for Foreman and left, Jessica spoke. "Okay, Foreman, we're here, talk to us."

"Hope you got time because it's a long story," Foreman said as he lifted the cup to his lips.

"We got time," Tyler replied.

"So you've met my wife, Monica, right?" he said to Tyler. "Well, a few years ago she developed a habit. She's tried getting clean…and even manages to for a while then something happens or she just gets the itch, you know, and is hooked again," Foreman said as he stared into his cup. "One day I'm at work and Cafferty approaches me. He asks if I'd be interested in making a little on the side, says he has a friend who could use some help now and then. At first I said no. I mean, I didn't want any part of it; my job is to put criminals away not help them."

"Well, it's supposed to be the job, yeah," Jessica said.

"Yeah, well another couple of months went by and here's Cafferty again, not so much asking me this time. He said he'd done some investigating and found out about Monica's problem. Hell, by that time he'd made sure he had one of Vargas's guys as her supplier. Cafferty said if I didn't help him and Vargas he would expose my wife's addiction. I just couldn't let him do that…I mean it would have destroyed Monica, the boys, so…Jesus, I can't believe I'm talking to you about this," Foreman said as he brought his hand to his eyes and gently rubbed with his fingers.

"Keep goin', Foreman, I didn't come here for only half of the story," Tyler spoke, his voice carrying the bitter disgust he felt toward the other man.

Jessica looked at Tyler with a frown and then to Foreman. When she looked at James she saw a man beaten down by the weight he had carried, and her voice held compassion when she asked, "What did he want you to do at first?"

"At first he just wanted evidence lost, reports to go missing…things I could easily slip into the evidence rooms and take. Then he wanted me to fill him in on planned raids, when requests were gonna be made for wiretaps…stuff like that."

"How could you turn on your fellow agents like that? Jesus Christ, you're responsible for Alverez's death," Tyler said his anger barely contained.

"Fuck, you don't think I know that?" Foreman said as he leaned into the table, almost in the other man's face.

"Easy boys, this isn't helping. Does Cafferty or the organization know about Luce having been undercover?" Jessica asked as a cold knot began to form in the pit of her stomach.

"No, Cafferty pushed me to give up the other agents, but I wouldn't. Velazquez is still in the clear."

"So why did you want to talk to us and come clean?" Tyler asked.

"Because I think he's gonna kill me. He's said on more than one occasion that my usefulness is about over. If I'm dead…so is the rest of my family. I'm tired of being blackmailed and I'm fucking scared."

"James, you could have come forward at any time before now. What happened that you had to call me at five this morning?" Jessica asked.

"Around midnight I got a call from one of my sources, a tip on where Beth Ryan is. Cafferty wants the head seat of the organization and he is positive that Ryan has information regarding all of Vargas's contacts and he needs them."

"So we were right, there's gonna be a power play from within," Tyler said as he looked at Jessica. "Do you know any of the other players?" he asked Foreman.

"He is pressuring for information on the Chameleon. Maybe he thinks he's involved somehow."

"This whole thing just got a lot bigger," Jessica said as she sat back rubbing her temple, a sure signal that a massive headache was developing. "Have you told him about the tip you got on Ryan?" she asked.

"Not yet, but I have to tell him something. He was at my home last night and made a point of telling me I have until this evening to give him something useful."

"Doesn't give us much time," Jessica said, looking at Tyler. "What did your source tell you?"

"He gave me an address in North Dakota, along with a phone number."

Glancing at each other the two agents both felt a sinking feeling in their stomachs, though they kept their faces neutral. It was possible that Beth's location was still secure, but it was a seasoned agent's intuition that screamed at them.

"Go ahead and make the call to the marshals, I'm not digging for confirmation; I'm trying to find a way out of this massive mess alive," Foreman said as he sat back, a look of utter defeat clearly showing on his face. With that, Tyler stood up and walked out the front door, heading to his car to make the call.

Jessica looked at the man who sat in front of her. "Is this what you wanted to talk about the other day in my office?" she asked.

"Yeah, but I panicked. Cafferty slinks around the place like the snake he is. I'm at the end of my rope…I just want this all to end."

"I can understand that. What do you think is gonna happen now?"

"Well, assuming I survive the night, at the very least I'll be facing a few felony charges. Look, Agent Sullivan, I'm not stupid. I know I'm responsible for more than one death, indirectly at least, and I've broken the law on more than one occasion. I came to you for two reasons: one because I want to get out of this alive, and two because my conscience can't take it anymore."

"Okay, you know for starters you are fired as of this moment. I can't promise anything but I'd think the mere fact that you're talking to us is a step in the right direction. I suppose the main question is how far are you willing to go to make this right."

"I'm willing to do whatever you say, just keep my family safe."

At that moment, the door opened and Tyler walked back in. With the barest shake of his head, he spoke to Jessica, "We need a plan and fast."

"Foreman, I need to know who your source is. I need to know where he or she gets his information."

"I won't give you that."

"You don't get it, do you, Foreman. Your source has access to information that is classified, information that is supposed to be in place for the security of others' lives."

"I'll think about it, but you're right, Tyler. We do need a plan and I need to know what the hell I'm supposed to tell Cafferty."

"We're gonna have to move fast, we have to set a trap. I'm assuming you alerted the marshals about the potential problem?" Jessica spoke.

"Yeah, they are sending some backup to cover Ryan."

"So the tip on her location was good," Foreman said as he nodded his head. He had known as soon as he heard the voice on the phone last night that the information was good. Hell, why else would he have called for this meeting? "So I tell Cafferty where Ryan is and you're all there when he comes to take care of her?"

"We don't know that he will be the one to show up. Somehow I don't think he does the dirty work, do you," Jessica said.

Foreman nodded at the comment. "You're right, so arrest whoever it is that shows up and press them to flip on him."

"Seriously, how long have you known Cafferty? Does he come across to you as someone that others would turn against? Especially being in bed with Vargas's organization, they aren't known for their tolerance, you know," Tyler said harshly.

"No, they aren't, but I don't want another death on my conscience," Foreman said as he ran his hand through his hair in frustration.

"Ya should have thought about all that before you got into bed with these assholes too," Tyler muttered angrily.

For the next few hours the three brainstormed and finally came up with something that resembled a plan. Foreman left before the agents, in case someone spotted him. Several minutes later when Jessica and Tyler walked out, Luce, still dressed in her disguise, approached them. Immediately Tyler stepped in front of Jessica, in a protective stance. "Back up, leave the lady alone. Here go grab you a nice hot meal," he said as he brought a twenty out of his front pocket. Jessica hid the smile as she looked away.

Luce mumbled thanks as she took the money and ambled toward the diner.

Chapter Fourteen

Foreman's thoughts raced as he drove home after his meeting with the two agents. He had done the best he could with what he had, he had made the best decision he could at the moment, and deep down he knew he was looking at some serious charges and probably jail time. He wondered if he was doing right by not giving them the name of his informant, if this plan they had come up with was actually gonna work, and most importantly he thought of his next steps. It wouldn't be long before Cafferty called wanting Ryan's whereabouts. Would he be able to maintain his composure and lie to the man? He had to, his life depended on it. His stomach clenched at the thought and it was all he could do to keep from getting sick on the spot.

"Just tell him what we came up with, it will be fine," he said as he pulled into his driveway. He had just turned off the engine, when his cell phone chimed. With the sinking feeling, he looked at the caller ID before he answered.

"I've been waiting for your call."

"I knew you would be, so what did you find out?"

"Ryan is in North Dakota, a town called Grand Forks. The address I have is 3466 28th Ave. South."

"About damn time you found something. Good, now I can get what I need. Thanks, James, looks like maybe your usefulness is still intact."

"I'm glad I could help out," Foreman replied as he closed his eyes and said a silent prayer of thanks, even as he knew if

Cafferty ever found out his role in this farce, he truly was a dead man.

"I'll be in touch, Foreman," Cafferty said and the line went dead.

Foreman looked out the window of his car. He needed to let Sullivan and Tyler know that Cafferty had the information, just as they planned. Taking a deep breath he dialed the number he had memorized. It was immediately answered. "I told him what you said to say. He's going after her, or sending someone after her. All he said was that now he would be able to get the information he needed. Yeah, I'll be in touch when I hear something more," he said and then hung up. He opened the door to his house and walked in. As he tossed his keys on the small table as he had the night before, he called out, "I'm home, Mon, and starved; what's for dinner?" For the first time in a while, he actually felt as if maybe there was some kind of light at the end of the tunnel.

✝

Amanda paced the floor of her apartment; her instincts were telling her there was a deeper story. So far, all her research had raised were more questions than it answered. The fact that Beth Ryan was involved with Judge Stone before his death wasn't suspicious; the fact that it appeared she left the judge to be with Vargas changed that picture a little bit. The fact that a collection of coins was stolen during the robbery in which the judge was killed and hadn't surfaced makes the robbery a tad fishy. There are many places coins could be disposed of for a good amount of pocket change. From what she was hearing, the collection had pieces that were sought after by other collectors, and with the right fence, those could be dumped in a heartbeat. "There's lots of money to be made with the sale of these coins, so…why aren't they being sold?" she said as she walked around the room, thinking. "Are you sitting on them because you don't know where to go with them or because they mean something to you? Or maybe you're hanging on to them for your nest egg later on. If that's the case then you more than likely have a job and weren't relying on the cash and coins from the robbery."

"Luce, I wonder if you're aware of Beth's connection to the judge," she said aloud and decided to pick up the phone. "Hi, it's Amanda, I was wondering if you'd like to meet for a drink or something. Yeah, I might have some information, if not I surely have more questions." She laughed into the phone. "Okay, sounds good. I'll leave now, see you soon."

†

Luce quickly grabbed the phone the second it started to buzz, hoping it was Jessica. She hadn't touched base with her since the meeting with Foreman. Whatever had happened, it sent Tyler racing to his car where he spent a good few minutes in a very animated conversation. She was disappointed when the voice on the other end of the phone was not Jessica's. The last thing she wanted right now was to go out, especially with someone that wasn't Jessica, but Amanda said she had some information, and right now she needed to know what that was. So, she grabbed her motorcycle jacket and headed to the garage where her Heritage Softail Harley was parked. Sliding her leg over the bike, she put on her safety glasses and helmet and rolled the bike out of the garage. She hit the button that automatically shut the door, and then pushed the button that brought the blue pearl-colored bike to life and roared off.

†

Amanda walked into the somewhat crowded pub, and looked for the tall, dark-haired woman. When she didn't see her went to the bar to order a martini and sat on the vacant

126

stool to wait for Luce. She didn't have to wait long, because about five minutes after she arrived, Luce walked in. Amanda couldn't help but smile when she saw Luce, and she felt a slight bristle of jealousy when she noticed more than a few women making a beeline toward her. Raising the martini to her lips she muttered to herself, "It's work, keep focused. Just keep focused."

"Hey, hope you didn't have to wait too long," Luce said as she took the empty stool beside Amanda.

"Not long," Amanda replied as she cocked her head and smiled. "What's your poison?"

"Actually, I'll just have a Coke."

"Really, I thought you were more of a scotch type of person."

"At one time…you read about my recent past, right? You know about the accident and…" Luce was just about to talk about Joe but stopped just in time.

"Yeah, I did."

"I was in a really dark place after that and I could easily go back there; so I usually try hard to not let that happen."

"So you don't drink at all? I thought I saw you drinking beer at Nagy's."

"Nonalcoholic beer, yeah, I'll have one or two now and then, and I'll have a glass of wine, once in a great while I'll have some whiskey. We aren't really gonna discuss my drinking habits are we," she said with a smile. "A Coke, please," she said to the bartender when he appeared. "And another of what she has as well."

Amanda laughed and said, "No, we aren't. I actually found some information and wanted to talk with you. Oh thank you," she said to the bartender as he placed their drinks in front of them. "Here, start a tab please."

As soon as he was gone, Luce picked up her glass and pointed to a vacant table. "Come on, let's go sit over there. We can talk better there." She stood up and let Amanda go before her then followed her to the table and pulled out a chair for her before taking her own chair.

"Thank you," Amanda said as she sat.

"So tell me what you found out."

"I want to ask, how well do you know Beth Ryan?"

"I met Beth a little over a year ago. We became involved about six months after that; I'm thinking I know her pretty well."

"Even though she was with Donavon Vargas? Wow, you're a brave one."

"Either that or plain stupid," Luce said, shaking her head.

"Right, and again how well do you know her? Did you know she was involved with a federal judge?"

"Jessica said something about that, yeah, but what does that have to do with anything? If she was it was a part of her past," Luce asked as she felt herself getting defensive.

"Shortly after Beth started being seen with Vargas, Judge Stone was killed in a home robbery, or at least that is the official version. I'm not buying that, though."

"Why?"

"Things aren't adding up. There were some valuable paintings that weren't touched. His office was trashed. I'm surprised the police were so eager to just let it go like they did. I saw the pictures, Luce; it looked to me like they were looking for something. The only things taken were some cash the judge had in his safe and a coin collection. Now who takes a coin collection? Wouldn't you think that whoever took it would have sold it?" Amanda asked.

"Well, I would think so…is it worth a lot?"

"Some coins are, yes; whoever has it is sitting on a small fortune."

"They haven't turned up…even on the black market?" Luce asked.

"No, not anywhere."

"Collectors are proud of their coins," Luce said as she thought about Beth. "I know Beth was very possessive of hers. Loved to show them off every chance she got."

That little bit of information sent Amanda's special sense crazy, but she was able to squash it. It wasn't that big of a coincidence that those two people would have a coin collection.

"Oh really…what did she collect, pennies, quarters?" she asked.

"Quarters, she loved quarters. She has one that is her pride and joy. I think it's an 1804 Draped Bust worth close to five thousand dollars."

Amanda's mind flashed on the copy of the police report she had seen—the one she couldn't wait to go over once more. If memory served, the judge collected quarters as well. All of a sudden this wasn't looking like such a coincidence. Not that she was ready to tell Luce that.

"You're the authority on this so you tell me what you think of my theory so far. Beth worked for the judge, I believe she was the office manager or something like that, I can't recall for sure, anyway, soon after, she becomes involved with him. At some point, she meets Vargas and realizes 'hey, this guy is loaded; he's handsome and much younger than the old man.' She starts flirting with him, puts herself in his path, maybe…I don't know, but either way she starts seeing him on the side. After a while, Vargas decides he doesn't want to share her, or she is tired of the judge and decides he has to go away."

"No…"

Putting her finger up in a silencing motion, Amanda continued. "Vargas had the connections, access to thugs of all kinds, and Beth decides to talk to one of them…boom, the judge is 'accidently' killed in his home during a robbery. Or maybe Vargas decides to keep Beth all to himself and arranges the robbery. Seems plausible to me, you tell me where the holes are."

"First off, Beth doesn't think that way, she isn't a cold-blooded killer. She wouldn't ever think about killing someone or having someone else commit a murder. Secondly, everyone makes her sound like a leech looking for a fresh blood supply. Tell me, how do you believe she met Vargas in this scenario that you've come up with?"

"Federal judge, top-notch criminal? It isn't a stretch to believe they crossed paths at some point in the courts."

"Okay, I'll give you that, you could have something there. But I know her; she couldn't kill a fly so I don't see her being responsible for the murder of someone. Now, do I think it's possible that Vargas got tired of the judge making demands on Beth's free time? Absolutely, and I do believe in a heartbeat that he would have the man killed," Luce said as she watched the beads of water roll down the glass in front of her. Her head was starting to hurt, and she really wanted a double scotch. She was missing something. Was it possible she didn't know Beth as well as she thought she did? No, she knew Beth, knew everything about her, and there was no way she was the monster everyone thought she was.

"Well, as you say, you know her. I don't. I may have also found where she is. Unless my source is wrong, and I'll tell you that's never the case, Beth is in North Dakota. I'm supposed to get an actual address soon."

"Does this informant of yours have a phone number to go with that address?" Luce asked.

"I'm supposing that I'll get that along with the address. Do you plan on calling her when you get that information?" Amanda asked.

"I don't know yet. Look, you know I'm sort of stuck here. Jess thinks Beth knows more about Vargas's organization than she's saying. If that's the case then it's my bet that there are a lot of people looking for her. That doesn't exactly speak of safe and sound to me, does it to you? At the moment, she has to feel like the entire world is after her and has no one to trust or nowhere to turn. Wouldn't you want to know there is someone out there who has your back and is looking out for you?" Luce asked.

"Well, of course I'd want that," Amanda replied. "You're a federal agent, you are the one that is supposed to protect and serve, make sure criminals are brought in and justice is served. Just consider for one moment that Jessica is right. What if Beth knows more than you think and your call makes her suspicious and she runs? Isn't that placing her in more danger? I'm sorry, Luce, I don't know you very well and I sure as hell don't know her, but my gut is telling me there is something that smells about her and the judge's death and my gut has proven to be spot-on about things like this."

As Luce thought about what Amanda had just said her phone vibrated in her pocket. Since she had been anxiously waiting to hear from Jessica she said, "Sorry, I need to see who is calling me." She pulled the phone out and mouthed, "I'll be right back" as she stood to head outside for a little privacy.

"Luce, I'm sorry, I just finally got a few minutes and wanted to let you in on what we found out from Foreman. It's what we thought, blackmail. We have the marshal's office doubling their men at Beth's location as we speak."

"Wait…what? You need to have them pull her back in if you think she is in danger," Luce stated loudly.

"Listen to me, no one feels she is in danger; this is more of a precautionary move than anything. Foreman says Cafferty just wants information on all of Vargas's contacts. So there's something to what I've been telling you about her knowing more than she's let on."

Luce's head was spinning and her stomach was in knots. Her doubts and the sudden untrusting feeling were all making their presence known, in fact, they were totally screaming. "I need to see you…to get this all straight in my head."

"Give me another thirty minutes to wrap things here, okay, then I'll meet you at your place, sound good?"

"Yeah, totally," Luce said as she walked back toward the pub's doorway.

"Luce…"

"Yeah?"

"Nothing," Jessica said as she pushed her thoughts aside.

Luce walked back to the table where Amanda sat and said, "Look, something came up and I need to get going. Give me some time to sort through what you've told me and I'll get back with you, okay? I'm real sorry about having to run like this."

"Oh, don't worry about it," Amanda said as she reached for her purse and stood up. "I'll walk out with you if you don't mind."

"Yeah, of course, I'm sorry, let me walk you to your car."

Chapter Fifteen

Cafferty's phone buzzed on the kitchen counter. He lay the knife down before grabbing a chunk of the bell pepper he had been cutting and popping it in his mouth. He wiped his hands on the dishtowel hanging from his shoulder before reaching for the phone.

"Cafferty," he said into the phone.

"I want a status on Ryan."

"I've got a lead and have my people on the way to secure her," he said as he felt his anger rise. He shouldn't be the one answering questions and the fact that he was just pushed all the wrong buttons.

"Good, I'll expect to speak with her in person by this time tomorrow. Well done, Cafferty, you just might be worth what I pay. I'll see you tomorrow, have a nice evening." The voice on the end of the phone chuckled before the line went dead.

Looking at his phone Mason could still hear the chuckle. Throwing it, the phone hit the wall and shattered. "Son of a bitch," he shouted. He put his hands on his hips and let his head fall back as he took a deep breath. He felt himself calm down. He focused on the bits and pieces of the device that were scattered on the floor. "Well shit, I suppose now I need a new phone," he muttered to himself as he walked to the broken phone. Bending down he reached for a bigger chunk and removed the micro SD card. He grabbed his jacket off the coatrack and the keys off the entryway table and headed out the door. Dinner would have to wait.

†

Jessica made it to Luce's place before Luce did, so she found the spare key and let herself in. She poured a drink as she waited for the agent to get home and let her mind wander. Her thoughts were all over the place. First and foremost, though, was putting this case to bed. It felt like all the pieces were falling into place, and once that happened maybe, just maybe, she could sort out her life. As she walked around Luce's home, she knew without a doubt she couldn't walk away from her ex-lover again. Try as she might she couldn't just forget about Luce, and God knows she had tried.

She was sitting on the sofa with her eyes closed, when she heard the front door open. "Hey, I'm sorry, I got here as soon as I could. What's happening?" Luce asked as she tossed the keys on the table and walked toward the sofa.

Rubbing her eyes, Jessica spoke, "Marshals should be securing her any minute. Foreman doesn't know it but there are eyes on him as well, and until Cafferty spots it there's a car outside his place too."

Sitting in the recliner, Luce watched Jessica. "You're positive Cafferty will make a move on Beth?"

"According to Foreman it was the next call Cafferty said he was going to make. Right now, we have everything in motion, people in place to keep Beth safe. I know you don't like sitting back and waiting but neither of us has much of a choice. Let me get you a beer, you look like hell," Jessica said. She walked into the kitchen and opened two bottles of Budweiser, handing one to Luce as she walked back to the sofa.

"Thanks. I'd forgotten how nice it is to come home to someone," Luce said as she lifted the bottle to her lips.

"Luce, we need to talk…about what happens after all this is handled."

"Okay, but I thought you wanted to wait until afterward," Luce said as she sat forward and rested her elbows on her knees.

"I changed my mind, it happens now and then," Jessica said with a wry smile.

"I'm listening."

"Where do you see us…you and me, when this is over?"

"I don't know, Jess. What I do know is that in all the years we've been apart, I haven't found anyone that has been able to make me forget about you. I hear a song, catch a whiff of the perfume you wore, and the feelings, the memories are so real I swear I'm living through it all over again. I think we are both more mature now, know what it takes to make things work and what it means to compromise. I think we owe it to ourselves to give this…give us another chance."

"And Beth? What about her? You know me better than to ever think I'd…"

"And you know me well enough to know I'd never ask let alone think about it. Look, I know I haven't officially broke it off with Beth, though I kind of think that's pretty much a given considering everything and where she is…I know if I can't trust someone I can't be with them, and I don't trust Beth. I suppose if I were being honest, I haven't trusted her in a while. I need to talk with her, let her know where I stand. What about you, where do you see us going? What do you want?"

"I've missed you. I think every relationship I've had since you hasn't worked because I measure all women to you, and none measure up. I…I don't know anything other than I can't keep living as I have. I want someone to come home to, not a damned empty apartment that I see maybe two days a week if I'm lucky."

"Is that all you see in me, someone that you come home to?" Luce asked.

"No…you know better than that. I want you to be the one I come home to, the one I wait for to come home, the one I fix dinner for or whatever. Look, I know the timing sucks and all with this case, but I miss you. I miss laughing with you and talking with you, feeling you next to me…god, I miss everything about you. I'm just so tired of fighting my heart and what I want…I can't do it anymore."

Luce got up from the recliner and placed her beer on the coffee table. She took the few short steps to the sofa where she sat down next to Jessica and drew her into her arms. She hugged the woman to her and whispered into her hair, "We'll figure this out, baby, I promise. You don't have to fight anymore."

Chapter Sixteen

The Chameleon sat back in his chair, a rocks glass in his hand, staring at the phone on his desk. With a sigh he spoke, "Mason Cafferty has worn out his usefulness. As soon as we get Beth back, he disappears…along with his associates."

"Yes, sir," came the response from near the door.

"She should be arriving in the next twenty-four hours. Make sure our plane is gassed and ready to depart. God willing, I won't have to see this godforsaken place ever again."

†

Cafferty was on his way home after getting his new phone when he spotted what he thought was a tail. He kept watch as he made several turns. Sure enough, though it kept at least a car length behind him, it was still there, making the same turns. Who put it on him, he wondered.

Cafferty ran all possible scenarios and his mind kept coming back to SAC Jessica Sullivan, that bitch from the ATF. He slammed his hand on his steering wheel. "FUCK, I knew something was going on, the bitch is investigating me!" he said in disbelief.

"How…what did she find, who said something to tip her off?" he asked aloud. "Foreman …that sniveling little fuck!" He stepped on the gas and shot out around traffic on his way to Foreman's home.

†

Jessica and Luce were sitting on the sofa discussing the future when Jessica's phone went off. As soon as she picked up she heard, "Agent Sullivan, Cafferty made the tail...he ditched them."

"Shit..."

"Agent, that's not all. We lost contact with the agents following him. We're thinking there was an accident; we heard what sounded like brakes squealing seconds before we lost the transmission."

"Damn it. Do we have a car outside Foreman's place? Any word on the condition of our agents?"

"Yes, the detail at Foreman's is giving an all clear so far. We have agents heading to the last known position of our men, and we're monitoring the local police feeds. I'll keep you up to date with information as soon as I hear anything."

"I think I need to come back into the office," Jessica said. "I'll be there soon as I can. God, I have a feeling it's gonna be one hell of a night."

"Yes, ma'am."

†

Cafferty drove toward Foreman's home as his rational side and his anger fought for control. He tried to think of anything he could have done to give himself away, to incriminate himself, and came up with nothing. Foreman had to have blown the whistle. "Okay, but you have to be smart about this...think, damn it. If they were tailing you, then they have a car watching that stupid fuck," he said to himself. "Now isn't the time to do anything stupid, think this through." After taking in a long breath of air and slowly releasing it, he headed home to plan and make some arrangements.

✝

Jessica hit the phones the minute she walked back into the office building. The command center was a flurry of activity. Agents on the phones talking to disconnected voices on the other end of the line, to each other. Fingers flew across keyboards as information was entered and retrieved. It was hours later when she got word on the condition of the men who were tailing Cafferty. One was in critical condition and the other, along with the driver of the garbage truck that hit them, was dead. When she finally got home she tumbled into bed exhausted.

On the other end of town, Cafferty was busy on the phone himself. He'd gotten word that Foreman's information was right and that his men had retrieved Beth. That was the first bit of information that made him smile, hell it was his first real smile in days. As he dialed a phone number the smile was still in place. "It's me. I'll have Ryan to you by this time in the morning. Do you want me to bring her to you?"

He got an angry response from the other end. "Are you serious? What else would you think I'd want you to do?"

That removed the smile. "I was just making sure," Cafferty said as the vein in his temple throbbed. "I'll let you know as soon she lands."

"You do that." Then the line went dead. For one angry instant Cafferty considered throwing his phone, but considering he had just dropped four hundred dollars on it, he thought better of it. Instead, he logged on to his computer and checked on outgoing flights. He didn't want to end things this way, he wanted more money in his bank account, but, hey, when it's time to go, it's time to go.

In less than twelve hours Mason Cafferty would disappear and somewhere in the world, Morgan Chambers would land. With a sigh of relief, he shut his laptop down, made sure his doors were locked, and turned out the lights as he made his way to his bedroom.

As he lay in bed, he thought about his course of action where James Foreman was concerned. He would like to make his death look like an accident, maybe a suicide, but the fact that he was sure the coward was being watched made it unlikely. He could almost see himself slipping into the house, arranging Foreman's 'suicide,' and slipping back out. He could see the fear in Foreman's eyes as he realized what was about to happen, and if by some chance Monica caught him, well, unfortunately, the fact of a druggie's life is an eventual overdose. "Oh, that would have been perfect…the perfect way for things to go. "Fuck it. If that bitch Sullivan has eyes on me, for sure they have someone babysitting that bastard," Cafferty said aloud as he stared at the ceiling. "No, I'll just have to wait and see what the situation is tomorrow morning. What's a couple of more dead bodies? The blame will go to Mason Cafferty and hey, guess what, Cafferty doesn't exist anymore!" he said as he laughed at his own joke.

✝

Cafferty woke the next morning with a sense of anticipation and a plan firmly planted in his brain. He packed what he thought he would need into a backpack then went into his bathroom, pulled out the box of hair dye and began applying it to his hair. Forty-five minutes later he looked into the mirror as he meticulously applied the spirit glue to the fake beard and mustache and placed them on his face. When he was done, the only thing he recognized in his reflection was his blue eyes. Gone was the blond hair and clean-shaven agent. "Goddamn, even my own mama wouldn't recognize me. Good-bye Mason Cafferty and hello Morgan Chambers," he said as he slowly dropped his voice an octave and added a southern drawl. He walked out of his bedroom, stopped at his desk to pick up the passport and fake ID, then walked out his back door.

As he made his way through the back gate of his fence he paid close attention to his surroundings, making sure he wasn't being watched. Once he was on the other side of the block, he caught a bus and headed to a garage where he kept a backup car. He looked out the windows, feeling the door of his past closing. Once he was in the old beat-up car, Cafferty drove to the airport where he purchased a ticket for later in the evening, and then he walked back to his car whistling, things were gonna work out just fine.

A few hours later was parked half a block away from the agents watching Foreman's place from a car parked across the street. With high-powered binoculars he watched, and thought, trying to decide how best to sneak in and rid himself of both Foreman and his wife. He watched the street, saw there was very little traffic and noticed how quiet the neighborhood was. All that had jobs were gone by now and from his experience homemakers did not spend their time looking out their windows. He reached for the baseball cap, which lay on the seat next to him, and put it on his head, pulling the brim down so that it hid his eyes just enough. He pulled his gun from the glove compartment and twisted on the silencer. With on final look up and down the street, he opened the door and stepped onto the sidewalk and headed toward Foreman's house and the agents who were watching it. Dressed in a jogging suit, Cafferty began a light jog; it was time to play the role.

"Isn't it a little late in the morning to be jogging?" the agent on the passenger asked as he observed the jogger in his side mirror.

"At least he's out joggin' instead of in front of some video game. Look at it this way—you get it in when ya can. Hell, there were days in the academy when I was up at four thirty in the morning trying to get my run in BEFORE my workout."

"Good point," the first agent said as he raised his paper coffee cup to his lips. He had just taken a drink when he heard a tap on his window. Putting the window down was the last thing he would ever do. The driver barely had a chance to look shocked before the bullet meant for him hit. Cafferty stood straight and once more looked up and down the street, pleased to see it was still clear. With a small smile he trotted up the driveway, glancing around now and then to reassure himself he was unseen.

He reached the front door and tried the doorknob. When he found it locked he reached into his pocket and pulled out his lock picks. It took just seconds for him to unlock the door and step inside. Quietly he made his way around and found Monica in the bedroom. As quietly as he could he reached into his jacket pocket and pulled out a cloth and small bottle of chloroform. He poured a small amount of liquid onto the cloth, put the lid back on the bottle and slid it back into his pocket. Then and only then did he slide behind the woman and clamp his hand over her mouth and his arm around her waist. In less than a minute she went limp. He laid her on the bed and went to work. From his other pocket he pulled out a needle and a rubber strap. He wrapped the strap around her arm and stuck the needle into her arm, gently pushing the plunger so the fluid flowed into her veins. Once that was done, he went in search of Foreman. He found the man in his downstairs office.

Foreman was sitting at his desk, simply staring at his hands when the door opened. Without looking up, he spoke, "Monica, this is my office. I'd appreciate it if you'd knock." It was then that he looked up and saw a stranger standing in the doorway with a silenced gun in his hand.

"Who the hell are you?" he shouted as he reached for the gun he had sitting on the side of his desk.

"No, I don't think you should do that," Cafferty said as he pointed the forty-five straight at Foreman's head. "Now James, I don't know whether to be pleased that you didn't recognize me or hurt that you cared so little that you never really paid attention. Sit your ass down," Cafferty said as he pointed the gun directly at Foreman's heart.

"What are you going to do? Monica is upstairs, she will be down soon."

With a deep laugh, Cafferty replied, "No…no, she won't. You see I've already paid her a visit. I'm sure she is…well, gone!" he said as he nodded his head and shrugged his shoulders.

"What did you do, Cafferty…Monica? Oh god."

"Will you just shut the hell up? How else did you think this would play out?"

"There are agents outside. Look, you can leave now and I won't say anything…Monica had a problem. It's that simple," Foreman pleaded.

"Seriously, do you think I'm an idiot? Those idiot agents aren't gonna be saving you, and I really can't just leave yet," Cafferty said. "You see, I'm not stupid. I know you blabbed and, well, you are the last loose end I need to tie up. Once I deliver that bitch Ryan, I'll disappear."

"You said all you wanted was to talk to her…you're gonna kill her, aren't you. Why, what did she do to you?"

"Really? You are asking me what she did? Okay, she didn't do anything," Cafferty replied. His eyebrows raised, his head nodding, as he spoke. "Honestly, I needed to know what she knows. I wanted Vargas's contacts. However, since I am leaving, I don't need them. The 'new boss' wants her, and I'm thinking I really don't give a shit what happens to her now. So, when my men get in, I'll deliver her and then I'm gone. Whatever happens to her from there is none of my concern. Now, I cannot even begin to tell you how much pleasure I'm going to get from this. You've been a real pain in my ass and

I'm so ready to be done with you," Cafferty said as he walked toward Foreman, the gun still aimed at his heart.

Foreman realized his luck had just run out and with a sigh of acceptance he sat back in his desk chair and prepared himself. If he had to voice his regrets, he supposed his biggest would be that he failed his wife. He couldn't keep her from destroying herself and he had tried, though maybe not hard enough, he thought. His final thoughts were of his sons and how they were going to feel when they found him and his wife, who lay upstairs, dead.

Chapter Seventeen

As Jessica walked through the doors of the office building, she felt the headache beginning. She walked into her office and placed her purse on the desk, digging through it for the bottle of aspirin. With two tablets in her hand, she walked back out and into the situation room where she loudly asked, "What's the status on Ryan?"

The answer from somewhere across the room, which had quieted a tad, was "Federal Marshals are on her, she was escorted out about four this morning. Luckily we were able to slip a tracker into her phone and purse."

"Good, what about Cafferty and Foreman?"

"After the accident, we had another team of agents head to Cafferty's house. He arrived around midnight, lights went out, and he hasn't left since," said another agent who stood by a desk.

"As of last report, which was thirty minutes ago, all was clear," another agent chimed in.

"Good, keep me up to speed on everything, do you hear me? We can't afford to screw this up."

Tyler came up to where Jessica stood and held out a cup of coffee to her. "I got a bad feeling about this," he said as he watched her pop two white tablets into her mouth and swallow them down with a sip of the dark liquid.

"Yeah, so do I," Jessica replied. "I told Luce last night about the conversation with Foreman. She was none too happy that we didn't just bring Ryan in."

"I've been thinking about that too. I gotta say, I'm wondering if we're doin' the right thing here."

"Hell, I don't know. What I do know is Ryan has information and is a part of this…and we have to find a way to put an end to Vargas's organization once and for all."

"I know, but is using Ryan the best way to do that?"

"I don't know…but I didn't hear you coming up with any ideas," Jessica grumbled.

"Hey, I'm on your side here."

"I'm sorry, I know you are and this is just…I'm just tired. I'm sorry for that comment."

"No problem, I understand where you're coming from," Tyler said as he turned and looked out at the room full of agents all doing something.

"Were we able to get a live tap on Ryan?" Jessica asked loudly.

"Yeah, a lot of 'marshal talk' reassuring her that she was safe from Cafferty's guys. She bought it and didn't resist." A rookie agent who was assigned to the communications part of the operation answered.

"Good. They should be arriving soon, so things will be happening fast. Is Cafferty still at his place?" she asked another agent.

"Yes, no movement on that end." With a nod of her head and a slight frown, Jessica turned her eyes to another agent.

"What about at Foreman's?"

"We haven't heard anything since the last check-in, maybe forty minutes ago," said a red-haired agent.

Jessica walked over to the agent, her stomach rolling with a sick feeling. She took the mike and spoke into it. "SAC Sullivan requesting update." She waited for a few seconds then repeated herself. "Something isn't right. Get a car out there and check on it."

"Agent Tyler we have activity on Ryan's end."

†

Cafferty had just sat down to a late breakfast at a diner when his cell phone buzzed. As soon as he heard the news, he tossed the napkin and enough money on the table to cover the meal he hadn't touched and a small tip. With a smile and spring in his step, he rushed out the door.

Inside his car, he dialed the number and as soon as the deep voice spoke he said, "I'll have Ryan to you in an hour."

"That is good news, Cafferty. I look forward to seeing you." Then the phone went silent.

"God, I can't wait to be done with this and never have to deal with you again, you son of a bitch," Cafferty said as he tossed his cell on the seat next to him.

†

A black sedan pulled up in Foreman's driveway and when the car doors opened, one man went to the front door and the other went to the car parked on the other side of the street. As the agent approached the car, he could tell things weren't right. He leaned down to look into the side window and his fears were confirmed. Turning, he rushed to the house and the agent who had been knocking on the door. "Bust it in, we got two down over there in the car."

"Oh shit," the sandy-haired agent exclaimed as he stepped back and kicked in the door. With their weapons drawn they cautiously entered the home. Moving through the house, they came to the office where they found Foreman at his desk, a gun with a silencer lay next to his hand. The scene before them stunned them for a moment before the agents moved through the rest of the house, making sure it was clear. They found Monica Foreman upstairs on the bed.

They made their way downstairs after doing a sweep of the house. The sandy-haired agent radioed in the situation.

At the situation room, the agent who received the information shouted, "It's bad at Foreman's. Both agents stationed in the car are dead and so are Foreman and his wife. Agents on the scene say the wife OD'd, Foreman lost it, killed the agents then himself maybe. There's a forty-five lying next to him."

"FUCK!" Tyler shouted as he turned to look at Jessica. "This just went to shit in a handbasket."

With her head throbbing, Jessica rubbed her temple. "I want a position on Ryan now, alert locals to have a SWAT team ready to take everyone the minute she stops," she ordered the agents in charge of communications. Turning to some nearby agents she said, "Agents are to move into Cafferty's now. I want him in this office in thirty and I don't give a damn how it happens. MOVE!" she shouted before turning on her heel and going to her office where she slammed the door.

She was on the phone pacing when there came a knock on the door and it opened. With a finger held up, she said into the receiver, "Yes, sir, I understand and I'll get it all to you ASAP." With the call ended, she placed the receiver on the cradle and said, "Please have some damned good news for me."

"Sorry, it's not. Cafferty wasn't there. He had to have slipped out somehow."

"How the fuck did that happen? What the hell are we, a bunch of bumbling idiots? I'll tell you what, that's exactly what we look like. I just got my ass chewed and I look like a fucking moron," she screamed at Tyler.

Tyler reached behind him and closed the door. "I get it, trust me. I'm waiting for that same call from my supervisor, so don't go taking it out on me. Near as we can piece together, he snuck out the back door and around the fence line to the other side of the block. He must have caught a bus or something. We're getting his picture out to all airports, bus and train stations. So far no one with his name has purchased any sort of ticket. Initial reports on his credit cards are also saying there is no activity. We have Tech setting up alerts to ping us the minute any one of his cards shows activity."

"And Ryan where are we with her?"

"Nothing much, she is getting ready to land in a few minutes. We have people at the airport ready to take them all into custody."

"Good. Let's go and monitor this cluster fuck. Jesus, I'm gonna be lucky if I walk away from this with a job."

"I take it Luce doesn't know what's happening, since she isn't here."

"Fuck, I forgot to call her. I can't deal with her can you?"

"At the moment she is fine where she is," Tyler said.

Together they walked out of the office and back to the situation room, which was buzzing with activity.

"The plane just landed and we're waiting for authorization to board."

"Good."

Time felt like it was at a crawl, and it seemed to Jessica that it took forever before she heard anything. The room had quieted down and the radio turned up so they could follow the officers and agents at the scene.

"It's a go. Let's go. Everyone boarding keep alert and remember there are civilians on board."

"Roger that."

The moments of silence stretched before they heard. "Subject is not onboard. I repeat subject is not onboard."

Jessica reached for the mike and said, "SAC Sullivan speaking, what do you mean she isn't onboard, where the hell is she?"

"We just got word that they were instructed by US Marshals to let them depart before we boarded."

"Find them...NOW."

Looking at Tyler, she said incredulously, "Can this get any worse?"

"At the moment, I wouldn't doubt it."

†

Cafferty leaned against the beat-up car as he watched the Explorer approach. He was almost free and wanted to get this over with. The minute the vehicle came to a stop, he straightened and took a few steps forward as the driver's side door opened.

"Any trouble?"

"What trouble there was we managed to lose, but I wouldn't spend much time with idle chat. The pilot told us there were DEA and ATF agents waiting on the ground to board the plane. We managed to convince them to let us deplane before they let them on, but I have a feeling it won't be long before they show up. I had a feeling I was being tailed but didn't see anything."

"Son of a bitch," Cafferty swore. "Okay, is she sedated?"

"Yup."

"Good, here is your payment. Don't spend it all in one place 'cause there ain't no more of that. It's been real," Cafferty said as he handed the man a duffel bag full of cash.

With a nod, the man took the bag and walked away with his partner who had waited by the SUV.

Cafferty went to the car to retrieve his backpack then trotted over to the SUV and jumped into the driver's seat. He drove straight to the old warehouse where the man he suspected was the Chameleon waited.

†

Twenty minutes later he stopped in front of the warehouse. Beth was slowly becoming coherent and able to

150

walk on her own. Cafferty opened the steel door and the two entered, greeted by a big muscle-bound man who walked them to the upstairs office. There sat the man he was to deliver Beth Ryan to. Cafferty hated the man, he hated the way he dressed in those handmade Italian suits, and the damn Cuban cigars he smoked. He hated the simple fact that he felt it should be him sitting in that chair and that he knew it would never be.

"I see you can actually carry out a plan," the dark-haired man spoke as he stood, his blue eyes sparkling. "Nice look by the way, I would never recognize you had we not been expecting you."

"Yes, I'm sorry it took so long," Cafferty said through clenched teeth. *I should put a bullet through your skull right now.*

Cafferty grabbed Beth's arm and pulled her toward him. "Come here, damn it. You have someone who really wants to see you," he said as his fingers dug into her skin.

"Let go of her."

With a glare, toward the tall man, he let Beth's arm go.

"Are you all right, my angel?"

"I am now. What the hell did your goons use on me?" she asked as she passed Cafferty. "I have a splitting headache. Carlos, I've missed you so much," she said to the tall man who walked toward her.

"Wait…what you know each other?" Cafferty said in confusion as he watched the two embrace. "You didn't really want her for information, did you. Jesus Christ you played me."

The man turned to look straight at Cafferty and said, "I don't recall ever saying why I wanted you to find her. However, if you need to know my reasons, it's really simple. With you using your resources, I didn't have to use mine. Anything that went wrong was on you, and my identity was kept under wraps."

"But…I don't understand."

"Did you really believe that Vargas ran the organization all on his own? Really? Donavon was intelligent but he didn't have all the connections. I worked behind the scenes with the biggest drug cartels in the world to secure what he needed, all he handled was here in the States."

"Who are you?" Cafferty asked finally.

Beth laughed at the confusion on Cafferty's face as she said, "Hmm, should we tell him?"

"Of course, he won't live long enough to tell anyone."

Hearing the words, Cafferty turned ready to run for the door, but ran right into the man that had led them upstairs and two more standing at the door. He knew he would never see the outside again.

"Carlos Estes, Donavon's half-brother."

"No, Vargas has no family...I would have known," Cafferty said in disbelief, his hand rising to the back of his neck where he rubbed the tight muscles.

"As much as you agents want to know everything, sometimes you don't. You see, our father wasn't such an honorable man. I suppose you could say he found it hard to resist a certain woman in our village, and it didn't matter that he was married. Donavon didn't know about me until we were grown and our father had passed. We realized we liked each other, and that we could...help each other's businesses. Maybe you've heard of me...I'm known as the Chameleon."

Cafferty's eyes grew big and his stomach sank...it was the last thing he felt.

"Clean this up," Carlos said just as the outer alarm sounded. "You know what to do," he shouted as he grabbed Beth's hand and ran to the hidden exit to make their escape. Among shouts from local and federal officers, the men left behind held their hands up in the air and immediately fell to the floor when told to do so.

†

Tyler and Jessica walked into the warehouse minutes later. The news that there was an unidentified body meant an even longer day for Jessica. This case had more twists and turns than she could have ever imagined.

"SAC, we can't find Ryan," she heard a fellow agent say.

"What…what do you mean you can't find her? We followed the signal from the tracker here," she yelled as the frustration she felt finally broke free. "Goddamn it, how the hell did she get away?"

"We don't know. The tracker points to here and hasn't moved. We have a purse over there, but nothing else."

"Goddamn it, we look like a shitload of Keystone Kops," she mumbled, and when the agent just stood there, she shouted, "What are you doing just standing there? FIND HER, and get me a damned ID on that dead man," she said as she turned and walked out of the warehouse.

Tyler followed her, knowing how she felt. Hell, he was grateful that he hadn't heard from his supervisor, knowing that it was coming and when it did, he had damned well better have something to tell him. "Sullivan, go home, go grab some coffee but get away from it for a few minutes, all right. I'll let you know as soon as we have something on Ryan and whatever the hell is goin' on."

"I can't. I need to let Luce know what's happened. I'm actually surprised she hasn't shown up yet."

"True, come to think of it, where has she been?"

"Off following some of her own leads, I guess," Jessica answered.

Chapter Eighteen

Luce spent the night thinking over everything she had heard from both Jessica and Amanda, and she had to admit there were a lot of holes in the story she'd heard from Beth. Maybe Jessica was right; maybe she didn't know Beth as well as she thought she did. Maybe Beth had lied to her just as she had done to Beth. "No, what I did was part of my job," Luce said into the dark room, even as the tiny voice inside said, "Yes, and sleeping with her was part of the job too." Frustrated she rolled over and punched at her pillow to make it more comfortable; sleep was gonna be hard to find she thought.

†

Early the next morning, Luce found herself reaching for her phone and looking for the business card with Amanda Murphy's number on it. She needed someone to work through all of this with; someone who didn't have or feel as if they had something vested in the outcome.

A sleepy-voiced Amanda picked up the ringing phone and said, "Hello."

"Hey, Amanda, it's Luce. I'm sorry for calling so early, I hope I didn't wake you."

"You didn't. I'm standing here waiting for the coffee to finish brewing. What can I do for you?"

"Well, I was doing some thinking, and I was wondering if you, by chance, have any pictures of the coins taken from the judge's robbery?"

"Yeah, of course I do, along with all the reports of the investigation," Amanda replied as her interest grew. "Why what's up?"

"Do you maybe want to have breakfast? I fix an amazing omelet with spinach, tomato, mushrooms, and cheese and pour a killer orange juice," Luce said.

"Sounds interesting. I'm always a sucker for orange juice." Amanda laughed. "Give me, oh say an hour?"

"Sure thing," Luce said. Feeling as if she was finally doing something, she gave the woman her address and they said their good-byes.

†

An hour later Amanda was knocking on the door with a messenger bag full of files and photos.

"Hi, glad you could make it," Luce said as she opened the door and stepped aside to let Amanda in.

"Thanks for the invite. I can't say I was exactly looking forward to the bagel that would have been my breakfast otherwise."

"Well, the kitchen is this way," Luce said. "How about a cup of coffee while I get the omelets going?"

"Sounds fabulous. Anything I can help you with?" Amanda asked as she placed the bag on the floor next to a chair.

"Nope, I have everything ready to go, so um, let's see…cups are in the cupboard above the coffeemaker. I have cream in the fridge or some powdered creamer, sugar is next to the coffeemaker," Luce said as she pointed in the direction of the things before she began pouring the egg mixture into two skillets that sat on the stove.

Amanda poured two cups of coffee and as she added some creamer to her cup, she looked around the kitchen. "You have a beautiful kitchen, do you like to cook?"

"When I get the chance to, yeah. It's hard when you're undercover for long periods of time you know," Luce replied as she gently flipped the omelet.

"I can't imagine how hard it would be to be gone from your home and the things you enjoy doing," Amanda said as she lifted the cup to her lips.

"It's all a part of the choices we make, I suppose. I really couldn't wait to get back here after I got released from the hospital. I come here and it just kind of recharged my batteries you know?"

"From what I see it's the perfect place to do that."

"It's getting there," Luce said as she looked around. She was proud of what she had done with the place. It was slowly becoming the place she'd always dreamed of having. She slid the omelet out of the skillet onto a plate then reached for the second plate. Luce carried them over and placed them on the table and pulled out a chair. "Come on, let's eat this before it gets cold."

"It smells amazing and looks just as good, I can't wait to taste it."

"Then by all means, dig in," Luce replied as she placed her napkin in her lap and picked up her fork.

The two ate and shared idle chitchat. True to Luce's word, the omelet was as good as she said it was and Amanda savored every bite. After finishing, Luce brought up the reason for their meeting. "So now that we've eaten, what do you say about getting on those files and figuring all of this crap out?"

"Sounds good to me. I have all the police reports I could get my hands on, but I'm wondering why you don't have them?"

Luce stood and with her cup of coffee in hand walked to the living room. "Honestly, until last night, I really didn't want to admit that Beth had been lying to me all along. Now, I want the truth. Some information is better than none, and you have access to it while it would take me some time to get my hands on it all."

"Okay, good enough." Amanda opened her oversized purse and pulled out a thick folder.

"Here are the photos the insurance company had on the coins. Like I said, no sign of the coins have shown up, and at this point I seriously doubt that they will," Amanda said as she handed the pages to Luce.

Luce looked through them, stopping on one image in particular. "Tell me how much of a coincidence is it for me to have seen two of these in my lifetime?" she asked as she pointed to the 1804 Draped Bust.

"I'm gonna say you should probably buy yourself a Powerball lottery ticket. The information I'm receiving is that coin is extremely rare. One in mint condition can be worth over $157,000 dollars."

"You're kidding me…right?" Luce said as she looked up at the redheaded woman, her face showing the shock she felt.

"Sorry, but yeah, that's what I'm hearing. And here's something else, the judge had that coin insured for that amount," Amanda said as she looked at copies of the insurance policies.

"This can't be happening," Luce said as she continued to look at the photo.

"The odds of Beth having a coin like this are astronomical, you know that, right?"

"Yeah, I know. I can't even begin to figure out how she could afford it."

"Maybe it was a gift," Amanda offered.

"From who, even the judge I bet had to do some penny-pinching to afford this. Her family, from what she told me, couldn't have afforded to get it for her, and Vargas, hell, he handed out the money she was allotted for the day, and insisted any jewels be in HIS safe when she wasn't wearing them. I'm not liking what I'm seeing here."

"You're starting to see what Jessica sees, aren't you?" Amanda said softly.

"I…yeah, I suppose I am. I've been doing lots of thinking on this, and something isn't working for me. This is just another arrow pointing to a bullshit story she gave me right from the start," Luce said as she tossed the photos on the coffee table. Truthfully she had no right to be mad or upset, she had lied about herself from the start. *Stop it, you were on the job. Beth just flat-out lied,* her little voice said.

"You up to some footwork?" she asked as she looked over to where Amanda still stood.

"Sure, where to?"

"I don't know, but I need to do something."

"How about we pay her sister a visit?" Amanda said as she reached for the papers, files, and bag.

"You found her? Everything I had was always a dead end."

"Yes, she lives here just outside the city. Come on, let's go for a ride," Amanda said.

✝

Forty-five minutes later the two women stood in a plush yard of green grass as they waited for their knock to be answered.

The door opened to reveal an attractive woman who looked as though she had just walked out of a photo shoot. Behind the dark glasses, Luce took in the woman from head to toe. Her hair was a light brown with auburn highlights that cascaded down in soft curls; her brown eyes held warmth and a trace of caution in them. As Luce's eyes traveled downward, she couldn't help but notice the woman had curves in all the right places. *Really? If Amanda is correct, this woman is Beth's sister and you're ogling her?* her tiny voice questioned.

"Yes, may I help you?"

"Hello, my name is Amanda Murphy, perhaps you've heard of me..." and when the woman shook her head she continued, "I'm an investigative reporter. Are you by any chance Susan Bauer?"

"Yes, I am, but why are you asking?"

"May we come in?" Amanda asked. "Oh, I'm sorry, this is Agent Lucinda Velazquez."

"Agent...I don't know what you would want to talk to me about," Susan said.

"Again may we come in, I'll explain everything inside."

"Mrs. Bauer, we're here to ask you about your sister, Beth," Luce said, cutting off anything Amanda was about to say.

"I don't know anything," Susan said as she backed up, getting ready to close the door on them.

"Look, I know you don't have any reason to believe me but I care about her and want to make sure she is safe," Luce said as she reached out to stop the door from closing.

"I don't...what do you mean?"

"Please let us come in, I'll tell you everything there," Luce pleaded.

Susan looked from Luce to Amanda then back to Luce and took a step back to let the two women in. "Can I offer you either of you some coffee?" she asked.

"Sure, that sounds great," Amanda said as she nudged Luce.

"Yeah, thank you. You have a beautiful home," Luce said, looking around from the entryway as she took off her sunglasses.

"Thank you," Susan replied. "Matt, my husband, has a good eye when it comes to decorating. I'll get the coffee if you want to take a seat in the living room."

Luce and Amanda walked into the room that Susan had pointed out. The room was tastefully decorated in tans and browns and felt very comfortable. Luce looked at the family pictures displayed on the walls and caught herself staring at the photo of two young girls. It had to be Beth and Susan when they were young children, she thought. She saw pictures of Susan and a man she assumed was Matt. She sat down on the sofa next to Amanda. "So what are you gonna tell her?" Amanda asked as she sat back and crossed her legs.

"As much as I have to, I suppose. Honestly, I hadn't thought that far ahead," Luce replied.

"Here we go. I didn't know if either of you take cream and sugar so I've brought both," Susan said as she walked in and placed the tray she carried on the coffee table.

"Thank you," Luce said, her eyes on the woman who sat down in the chair across from the sofa.

"You know Beth, don't you." It was more a statement than a question. Susan's eyes locked on to Luce.

Luce couldn't hold Susan's eyes and looked away. "I couldn't help notice the family pictures you have up on your wall. You and Beth looked very much alike as children."

"I always wanted to be like her when we were little…always looked up to big sister, you know?" Susan said. "How do you know her?"

"I met Beth a year ago, and we became friends," Luce said as she skirted the full truth.

"Beth isn't friends with women, or at least she wasn't…wait, you're her, aren't you?" Susan said as she sat forward in her seat and recalled what Beth had told her a few weeks ago, before she disappeared yet again.

"What do you mean?" Luce asked as her eyes snapped back to Susan's face.

With excitement Susan said, "Oh my god, you are! Look, I haven't seen Beth for a long time; she had a way of coming and going. Anyway she turned up about a month or so ago, told me she had met the one she was meant to spend her life with. Apparently that's you," she said as she looked at Luce.

"What else did she say?" Luce asked.

"Are you the woman she was talking about?"

"Yes…now what else did she say?"

"That was it. I mean, we caught up and then she left. She promised she would call and we would do dinner, but that was just another lie, I suppose," Susan said.

"Susan, Beth has been in protective custody. The man she was with, Donavon Vargas, was a very bad man," Luce began.

"I know about Vargas. I couldn't believe she would risk coming here and exposing us to danger like she did. However, she swore she wasn't followed and that he didn't know about us. I suppose I was really stupid for not asking to see some credentials or something before inviting you in," Susan said in hindsight. "I read that Vargas was dead, so I thought the danger was over."

"Susan I need to ask you some things about Beth," Luce said.

"What can I tell you that you don't already know?" Susan asked as her eyebrows shot up in confusion.

"I know this is hard, but Beth never really talked about her past and childhood. Everything I know right now is… I am having a hard time deciphering what is real and what isn't."

"Unfortunately Beth has that problem. What do you need to know, Agent Velazquez?"

"Has Beth always collected coins?"

"She didn't. Beth didn't have the patience for things like that. If it didn't provide instant satisfaction she wasn't interested."

"I see," Luce said thoughtfully. "She never mentioned becoming interested in it as an adult?"

"No. Did you ever see Beth interested in anything more than spending money?" Susan asked. "Look, I may not have spent a lot of time around Beth but, trust me, Beth isn't hugely different as an adult than she was as a child."

"Were you on speaking terms with her when she was working for Judge Marcus Stone?"

"She worked for a judge? I'm sorry, its just…Beth wasn't ever very committed to working," Susan said. "She played you, didn't she, Agent? I'm sorry, I wish I could help out more."

Susan had just finished speaking when the front door opened and a man said loudly, "Hey Sue it's just me. I forgot…uh, what's going on?"

"Matt, this is Agent Velazquez and Amanda Murphy. They're here asking about Beth," Susan said as she stood up and walked toward the man. "This is my husband, Matt."

"We don't know anything and haven't seen her in months. So if you don't mind let me show you to the door," Matt said as he held his hand toward the entryway and the front door.

"Mr. Bauer…" Luce began only to be cut off by Susan.

"Matt, I want to help."

"Help how? We didn't know anything about her life or her," Matt said, his voice holding a trace of the anger he felt each time he heard his sister-in-law's name.

"Oh, stop it," Susan snapped. "I'm so tired of how you behave when you hear her name or anything to do with her. Whether you like it or not, she is my family. Maybe not the kind you think I should have or the kind you want, but that doesn't change anything."

Matt Bauer was shocked at his wife's outburst and his expression showed it. "Babe, I didn't mean—I hate how she just pops in and out of our lives with no thought of what happens when she vanishes."

"Mr. Bauer, how well did you know Beth?" Luce asked. The fact that Matt Bauer didn't like Beth hadn't escaped her and she wanted to know why.

"I didn't. Look, Agent Velazquez, is it? Beth was never what I would call sister material. She didn't care about anyone other than herself and only showed up when she needed something, usually when she was in trouble," Matt said as he turned and looked at Luce, his hands on his hips.

"What do you mean she only showed up when she needed something?" Luce asked.

"No, I don't need to explain anything," Matt said as he shook his head.

Luce looked to Susan. "You said she had a way of coming and going, before last month, when was the last time you saw or heard from her?"

"I don't know…why?"

"Mr. Bauer, how about you?"

Matt's face grew red. "I…what damn difference does it make?"

"Matt?" Susan asked, her hand reaching out to touch her husband's arm. "You would have told me if you'd seen or talked to Beth right?" When her husband refused to look at or answer her, she continued, "Matt, answer me."

"Sue, she didn't care about anyone, including you," Matt replied as he tried to explain his position. He thrust his hands toward his wife. "All she ever wanted was money. Why would I tell you that? How could I tell you that I'd heard from her or saw her and she never once asked about you, never once wanted to see you?"

"Oh, my god, you make it sound like this happened all the time," Susan said with a mixture of shock and pain.

"Sue, I'm sorry. I should have told you but…"

"How often did it happen?" Luce asked, effectively stopping further conversation between the two.

"When we were first married she called at least once a month then less frequently."

"Did she ever mention a boyfriend or anything?"

"Not to me, no, but there was something that didn't make sense. Maybe about two years ago she asked me what I knew about old coins. Hell, she even asked if I knew any collectors."

"Why would she ask that?" Susan asked.

"I don't know," Matt replied. "Susan, I'm sorry. I should have told you. I just didn't know how to tell you."

"She loves me, she just has…is there anything else, Agent?" Susan asked as she wrapped her arms around herself as though she were cold.

Amanda stood up and, reaching for her purse, said to Luce, "Come on, I think we've taken up enough of Mrs. Bauer's time."

Luce nodded as she stood. "Of course. Mrs. Bauer, I'm sorry for…well, for everything." She stopped midstep and continued, "Uh, in answer to your earlier question, yes." She reached into her back pocket and pulled out a card case, retracted one and held it out. "Here's my card. Please feel free to call with any questions you have…I promise I'll try to answer them."

Susan reached for the card with a slight nod. Matt led the way to the front door with Amanda behind leaving Luce to catch up.

Chapter Nineteen

Luce and Amanda had just gotten into the car when Luce's cell phone buzzed. Pulling it out she answered, "Hey, what's up?"

"Where are you? We need to talk," Jessica said as she walked briskly to her car and slid in, leaving Tyler at the warehouse to finish things there.

"We're just leaving Susan Bauer's, uh, Beth's sister. What's up?"

"We?" Jessica asked curiously then dismissed the question. "Things are happening. Foreman is dead and Cafferty is in the wind."

"What do you mean, what the fuck happened, what about Beth, is she still under the marshals' protection?" Luce paused and listened, before uttering, "Shit, I'll be at the office soon as I can make it." As she disconnected the call, she looked at Amanda and said, "I need to get to the office. Can you drop me there?"

"Of course," Amanda said as she started the car and pulled out on the street to head back to the city. The entire ride in, Luce went through what she had heard from Matt Bauer. Why in the hell would Beth ask about coin collectors?

"Penny for your thoughts," Amanda said, hoping to break the silence.

"Way too many thoughts, but the main ones would be, why was Beth asking about coin collectors? Why did she hang on to that coin? Did she know how much that coin was worth? Hmm, the bigger question is the personal one, and that's just not professional but it's still right up there, ya know…Christ, did I really not know this woman?"

"Sounds to me like she definitely kept things from you, but then again you weren't all that honest with her either."

"That's not fair; I was on the job that means undercover."

"Ah yes…and part of that means sleeping with an individual directly involved with the subject of the operation," Amanda replied softly.

"Yeah, I know, not the smartest thing I've ever done," Luce uttered as she turned and looked out of the side window, wishing for nothing more than a double scotch on the rocks at that moment.

"So, you know I have to ask, what's going on? I couldn't help but hear the tone in your voice," Amanda asked. She took her eyes off the road and looked at her passenger. She could tell that Luce was worried by the clenching and unclenching of her jaw.

"Can't talk about it, especially to a reporter, sorry," Luce said as she turned and looked at Amanda.

With a sigh Amanda said, "Just don't forget about our agreement. I still have dibs on the exclusive." With a wink and a smile she turned her attention back to the road. Both women were lost in their own thoughts as they finished the ride in silence.

✝

With promises to call, Luce said good-bye to Amanda and ran into the building. With brisk steps she went straight to Jessica's office, and without even knocking, walked in. "What the hell is going on? What's the latest on Cafferty, did you find him yet?"

Jessica raised her head from the computer monitor, closed her eyes and shook her head. "All hell's broke loose. We had a car on Foreman and Cafferty. Last night Cafferty spotted our people, but lost them when he sped up at an intersection and the agents following him were slammed into by a garbage truck."

"Oh Jesus, how are they?" Luce asked the concern heavy in her voice.

"As of two hours ago one is still in serious condition…we lost Agent James at the scene last night."

"Well, fuck…" Luce said as she ran her fingers through her hair. Then she took a good look at Jessica. "Have you taken anything for your head?"

"I've been popping aspirin like candy, it's not helping," Jessica replied as she rubbed at her temple.

Luce stepped behind Jessica and gently placed her hands on her shoulders. Softly her fingers began rubbing up the neck toward the base of Jessica's head.

"Luce, don't this isn't…oh god, that feels good," Jessica said as she let herself enjoy the contact of Luce's hands and the feel of the motion on the tight muscles.

"Relax, I'm just a colleague trying to help out. You let it go too long and now it's a full-blown migraine isn't it?" Luce asked as she applied a little more pressure with her fingers.

"Yeah."

"How about your pain pills, do you have any?"

"Not with me. I've been so wrapped up with things here I forgot to grab them when I did get home for a few minutes."

"Have you eaten anything? Do you think you can keep anything down if you do eat?" Luce asked, the concern and worry once again evident in her voice.

"I can't remember the last time I ate. I think I can keep food down," Jessica answered.

Luce walked back around Jessica and went to the door where she scanned the room. "Hey Maggie, can you please run to the diner and get a grilled cheese sandwich and some of their extra bold coffee."

Luce had just turned back into the office and was walking toward the vacant chair when there was a knock on the door and Tyler stuck his head in. With a groan at seeing Luce, he turned to look at Jessica and said, "You're gonna want to hear this," and tipped his head toward the situation room. Jessica stood up and walked toward the door with Luce following behind her.

Tyler walked into the command center and waited for the two women to join him in the room. "Listen up," he shouted and waited for the room to quiet down. "We found Cafferty. We got a hit on prints from the body at the warehouse. They came back as Cafferty's. Just to make sure I had them run again. It's him."

"Shit," Jessica uttered, her headache getting worse, if that was possible.

"What about Beth Ryan? Anything on her?" Luce asked as she stood behind Jessica with her arms crossed in front of her chest.

Jessica could feel the anxiety radiating from Luce.

"The tracking device the marshals managed to slip into her bag was found along with her purse at the warehouse, other than that there's nothing. We have her picture out to law enforcement, bus, train, airports…we'll find her."

"Right, but will we find her alive?" Luce asked then turned on her heel and walked out of the room.

"Did you find anything else?" Jessica asked.

"Keys on the body led us to an SUV outside where we found a laptop, a wallet with credit cards, a picture ID of the victim and a receipt for a long-term parking garage. We have techs going through the laptop as well as going through charges on the credit cards."

"Keep me updated," Jessica said as she left the room and went to her office, hoping that's where Luce went. Jessica walked in just as Luce was taking the wrapped sandwich out of the paper bag.

Jessica walked to her desk as she looked at Luce. She couldn't get a read on the woman and it was starting to worry her a little. She took her seat as Luce walked toward the large window and stood with her hands in her pockets, looking out at the city.

"You're worrying me. What's going on in your head?" Jessica asked.

"I woke up this morning realizing I needed to look at this whole thing with Beth without the blinders. I called Amanda Murphy and we got together for breakfast and went over what she has found in her investigation. It seems the judge was very interested in collecting old coins, quarters to be exact. He had one coin estimated to be worth more than $157,000 dollars. We, Amanda and I, had just left Susan's house, Beth's sister, when you called. Did you know that up until that conversation with Susan, I believed that I knew Beth?"

"Okay and now?" Jessica asked as she took a bite of the sandwich.

"Now, I believe your theory on her involvement in that judge's death isn't so far-fetched. According to Matt Bauer, Susan's husband, Beth had asked him if he knew any coin dealers or collectors. Strange behavior for someone who doesn't collect, don't you think? Hell, according to Susan, Beth didn't have much interest in anything that didn't involve spending money," Luce said as she walked casually to the sofa placed next to the wall and sat down. "You know it kills me to admit that I let her fool me, that I was so blinded by what I thought she was that I didn't pay attention to what was right in front of me."

"What was that?" Jessica asked as she put her elbows on the desk and laced her fingers together in front of her while she waited for the answer.

"A player, a user, maybe a money-hungry leech. I don't know. Just not the sweet innocent girl she led me to believe she was," Luce replied. "I'm sorry I didn't listen to you, that I put it all on you being jealous or whatever. I never should have doubted you."

Jessica sat back in her chair watching the raven-haired woman in front of her. It was surprising to hear Luce admit to being wrong about anything without a trace of anger or some kind of grudge.

"Relax, Jess, I haven't gone off the deep-end I promise," Luce said with a chuckle.

Taking a breath Jessica nodded and said, "Okay, now what? You know the chances of finding Beth, especially if she is with someone in the Vargas organization and in hiding, are slim."

"I know, which means there is a whole new problem with much bigger ramifications," Luce said calmly as she leaned forward and put her elbows on her knees.

Feeling her stomach sink and her head begin to pound again, Jessica asked, "What problem?"

"Well, if I hadn't been made by the organization before I shot Vargas, I gave myself up to Beth that day."

"Wait, you did what? I'm sorry I believe I heard you wrong…I thought I heard you just say that you told Beth you are a federal agent and that you had just brought down a major arms and drug dealer who, by the way, happened to be her lover as well."

"Yeah, I sort of did."

"Jesus Christ, Lucinda! Have you lost every goddamned strand of common sense you had?" Jessica shouted, pushing away from her desk. She walked around the room with her hands on her hips as a million scenarios rushed through her head.

"I thought I knew the woman and I trusted her. I made a mistake," Luce said quietly.

"Right," Jessica said as she picked up the phone and punched in a number.

"Who are you calling?" Luce asked.

"US Marshals, you need to go into witness protection."

"Now wait a minute. We don't know that they are going to come after me," Luce argued.

"We are not having this argument," Jessica said as she pointed a finger at Luce. "Yeah, this is Special Agent Sullivan with the ATF. I need to arrange for witness protection for another agent. All right I'll be waiting."

"I'm not going into hiding," Luce said, standing up.

"I said I'm not arguing about this. We don't know where that bitch is. I've lost Joe and I'll be damned if I lose you too," Jessica said through clenched teeth.

"Look, I know one thing about Beth for sure, she has to have the last word. We stand a better chance of catching her with me in the open."

"So you're going to be bait…is that what you're telling me?"

"Bear with me. Beth is on the run and the last time I spoke to her, she sounded pissed. She blames me for Vargas's death and is damned sure that you and I are sleeping together. Right now, I'd bet she is pissed beyond belief. She blames me for Vargas, for losing her place in the money flow she had there. She probably feels I played her, which I did, but that's beside the point. I'd bet my life that she is going to come after me. Let her because I can take her down and I'll be damned if I live the rest of my life hiding from her."

"No, I won't let you do that," Jessica said as the anger she felt coursed through her blood.

Luce stood up and walked toward the door. "We'll talk more later. You need to get some rest and I'm gonna head home for a little while. I need to process things."

"Lucinda, I'm not done," Jessica said just as the phone on the desk started to ring.

Luce stopped and said, "Did you know there are only two times you call me Lucinda…when you're mad at me, or when you're about to come." She walked out with a smile while the phone continued to ring. "Better get that!" she hollered.

Chapter Twenty

While Jessica filled in her boss, Luce flagged down a cab for the ride home, thinking on the ride there about what her next step should be where both Beth and Jessica were concerned. The case Jessica was sent to town for was over, at least that's the way Luce saw it. Her relationship with Beth was also over. So she was free, and she was tired as hell of fighting her feelings for Jessica. As she thought about all the relationships she'd had since Jessica, she realized they all had been missing one thing: that connection, that spark that she had with Jessica. She realized that she never really opened up, never gave a hundred percent of herself to anyone…not since Jessica. She was tired of living life that way. She was done hiding half of herself and pretending to be happy.

Yes, Jessica, it's time we got our crap together and live happily ever after, she thought to herself just as the taxi pulled up to her house. She paid the driver and was just about to unlock her door when her cell phone rang. Without really looking she answered.

"Hello, Luce," Beth said. "Did you miss me?"

"Beth, I was just thinking about you," Luce said as her mind scrambled to make a plan.

"Oh yeah? That makes me happy. What do you say we meet somewhere, I miss you." Beth all but purred into the phone.

"Okay, I'd like to see you too," Luce said. "Where, and what time?"

"What about now? I'm at the Broadmoor, on 187th Avenue, Room 337."

"Oh you're in town?"

"Come on, Luce, I'm dying to see you."

"All right, sweetheart, I'm on my way," Luce said, praying she had been convincing enough. She quickly walked to the garage and her car.

†

Carlos sat with his feet propped up on the coffee table and a drink in his hand as he listened to the plans Beth made. "Why must you meet with this woman? Let's just go, my plane is waiting as is the villa in the South of France."

"Carlos, first off, I want to thank you. I don't know how I would have been able to continue living in that godforsaken place," Beth said as she walked over to where the man sat and curled up against him. "I just want to thank Luce for…well, for taking such good care of me. Donavon made a good choice picking her as my bodyguard."

"Please, we both know she was more than a bodyguard, and while I make no judgments let me be clear when I say I won't be made a fool the way Don was."

"Oh, sweetheart, you know I could never do that to you," Beth replied as she leaned in to kiss the man. "I just want to say a proper good-bye is all…I owe her, at least I feel as though I do. So please, all I need is a few hours, then I'll meet you at the airport and we can fly away."

"Very well, but let me leave one of my men."

"No, I'll be fine, I promise. Besides you need all eyes on you to keep you safe. I don't trust that fool Cafferty to not have let something slip about you. He was a complete idiot."

"Yes, you're right, he was foolish. Okay, I'll head to the jet, finish my business and then we can leave as soon as you get there," Carlos said as he swung his feet off the table and

174

stood. He placed the glass he'd been drinking out of on the dark wooden table and walked to the door where he slid on his shoes. Beth walked with him. He turned to her and wrapped his arms around her. "Do not make me wait too long," he said before placing a kiss on her lips. He reached for the doorknob and strolled out.

Beth's gaze followed him as he walked to the elevator, the smile on her face fading quickly as she closed the door. "Don't make me wait too long…please, I'll make you wait as long as I damned well want. Once I meet all your contacts and charm them, I think your usefulness to me will come to a fast end. I wonder if Luce would be willing to put a bullet in you as well?" She laughed at her little joke, and then said to herself, "No, I do indeed owe Luce." She went to the bedroom to begin her preparations for Luce's visit.

✝

Luce drove to the address Beth had given her, knowing she should have backup, but never making the call. About forty-five minutes later she was pulling into the underground parking lot of the hotel where Beth was staying. Luce stepped out of the car and walked to the elevator of the hotel. She pushed the button for the third floor and, with her hands in her pockets, took a deep breath and closed her eyes as she rode up. When the elevator stopped and the doors opened, she briefly wondered if she should have called for backup. She stepped out, looked both ways down the hallway then turned left as she looked for the room number Beth had given her. Finding the room Luce knocked. When the door opened, she found herself looking at the blond, green-eyed woman she thought she was in love with.

Luce looked the woman up and down and with a smile said, "You look fantastic," hoping as she said it that her true thoughts and feelings weren't visible.

"So do you, tiger," Beth replied as she took a step toward Luce and wrapped an arm around the tall woman's neck and brought her head down for a hot kiss.

The kiss took Luce by surprise and it was with effort that she managed to suppress the urge to push the woman away from her. Luce pulled her mouth from Beth's and calmly said, "Let's take this inside away from prying eyes."

"Good idea," Beth said, stepping back to let Luce in. As soon as Luce was inside, she closed the door and wrapped her arms around her again. "It's so good to see you again. I can't tell you how much I missed you."

"I know. I missed you too, and I can't tell you how glad I am to see you," Luce said as she slid back into her role.

"Did you really, baby? I was so sure that bitch, Jessica, had worked her way back into your bed," Beth said as her fingers played with the hair on the back of Luce's head.

"No, she tried, but you know I only have eyes for you, sweetheart," Luce said.

"Mmm-hmm, it's not your eyes I've been worried about, baby," Beth said as she leaned in to kiss Luce once more. Luce accepted the kiss but kept it short by pulling back and pretending to take a great interest in the décor of the room. "Wow, this is a fantastic room. How long have you been here?"

Dropping her hands, Beth trailed behind Luce who was walking around the room. Luce's eyes took in everything. She noted the closet as she was walking toward the sliding patio doors that led to the balcony. Luce opened them and took a step out. Satisfied that no one was waiting there to ambush her she walked back in and smiled at Beth who had been watching her.

"What are you doing, Luce?" Beth asked as she leaned on the back of the sofa with her arms crossed.

"Nothing, honey, I'm just admiring your choice of rooms," Luce said as she tried to keep her tone cheerful.

"If you say so. How about a drink and we can catch up…on everything," Beth purred while her fingers softly moved up Luce's arm.

"Yeah, that sounds really good," Luce said.

"Why don't you sit down, take your shoes off and get comfy. After a glass of wine we'll get even more comfortable," Beth said as she added a little more sway to her hips as she walked to the bar, knowing that Luce was watching.

Luce was indeed watching, wondering how she could have read the blonde so wrong. Now as she watched Beth all she could see was a woman used to getting what she wanted by any means possible. Before she could stop herself she asked, "Beth, why did you sleep with me…start a relationship when you had everything Vargas could provide."

Beth was surprised for a brief second, but recovered. *Okay, so the gloves are off,* she thought. "Well, I suppose I could tell you that you were just so irresistible and I couldn't withstand your charms. I could say that I was attracted to your amazingly trim and fit body, which by the way is true, but I suppose you want the truth, don't you?" Beth said as she walked back to the sofa with the glasses of wine. She handed one to Luce and then sat down next to her with the other one. She took a sip and placed the glass on the table, then turned to face Luce. "Come on, take a drink, it's your favorite," she said.

Luce picked up the glass and drank. Beth was right it was her favorite so she took another drink before setting the glass down.

"I'm waiting," she said as she sat back into the sofa.

"Well, Luce, I do find you extremely attractive, your body is to die for, and I had fun with you. But the honest truth…I was bored and you were a new toy."

Luce reached for the wine again and took another drink as she thought about what Beth had just said. "So the reality of things is you would never have left Vargas for me."

"Well, if it makes you feel any better, I did think about it. But then you told me you were one of those federal agents that hated him so much, and then, well, you shot him. I suppose that sort of changed my mind."

Luce who had been listening intently was finding it harder to concentrate on what Beth was saying, things started getting blurry. Luce tried to stand but only succeeded in falling over as the fog overtook her brain.

†

Jessica had spoken with her supervisor, given her a verbal report on the events that preceded both Cafferty's and Foreman's deaths, and her findings that the leak in the departments was from the two men. All she needed was to formally submit her written report, along with a few other things and this case was put to bed. Her migraine was finally dissipating, and with the case over, she could clearly think about her future. "What kind of future if Luce is dead set on being bait to bring Beth out of hiding?" she mumbled as she put the last file into her briefcase.

The knock on the door brought her out of her thoughts. "Come on in."

Tyler opened the door and walked in, his hands in his pockets. "How ya doin'?" he asked as he looked at Jessica.

"I'm doing all right. In fact, I just got off the phone with my supervisor, and I'm wrapping up the case. How about you?"

"Pretty much the same. Got a little ass chewing for the cluster fuck of last night and today, but as I told him there was no way we could have predicted all of Cafferty's moves. He was always two steps ahead of us."

"Yeah, he was. Did the computer guys get into Cafferty's laptop?"

"Yeah, we have bank accounts, dates, hell, we even found a safe deposit box where we found stacks of files and evidence from cases going back to when he started working here."

"Do you think he knew Vargas before?"

"It's looking that way," Tyler replied. "But who the hell knows."

"Did you find anything on Foreman?"

"No, we're still going with the idea that Cafferty was blackmailing Foreman. With all the needles and crap, we found, it's a damned good bet that he was holding that over Foreman's head. It doesn't look very good for a DEA agent to have a junkie wife."

"I suppose not. Jesus, he could have done something other than letting drug dealers and gun runners run free," Jessica said as she stood up from her desk and walked to the credenza and the water pitcher. She was pouring a glass when her cell phone went off. She walked with the glass to her desk and looked at the caller ID screen. The number was unknown, which made her frown, but she answered it.

Tyler couldn't help but notice the look on the agent's face, and he listened to the side of the conversation he could hear without appearing to listen.

"Yes, I can be there in thirty minutes, will that work? Fine, I'll see you then," Jessica said as she ended the call.

"Heading out?" Tyler asked.

"Yeah, I'm going to meet up with an old friend before I leave town," Jessica said as she reached for her purse and opened the drawer of her desk where she kept her Sig. She put the gun in her purse, and with keys in her hand, slung the purse over her shoulder.

"Well, okay, I'll see you later then…you will come by the office again, right?" Tyler said as he walked Jessica out.

"Yes, of course I will." Jessica smiled. She walked toward the double doors and her car outside. Tyler waited for about a minute, his eyes never losing sight of Jessica, before following her outside and getting into his car.

"An old friend…Jessica, really, do you think I'm stupid?" he said as he drove. Something didn't feel right. He didn't like her body language when that call came in and he didn't like the tone in her voice as she spoke to the caller. It didn't add up to being a conversation with 'an old friend.'

He cautiously followed her to a hotel called the Broadmoor. He watched her get out of the car and enter the elevator. He ran into the lobby and watched the elevator go up to the third floor. He looked for the next elevator heading up and ran for it, just barely sliding in before the doors closed. He punched the third-floor button and felt the adrenaline kick in. As soon as the doors opened, he looked up and down the hallway and spotted Jessica entering a room.

He walked down the hallway briskly and listened at the door.

†

"Hi, Jessica, I bet you never thought you'd be seeing me again, did you?" Beth said as she closed the door behind Jessica.

"Actually, I knew I'd see you again. I had just hoped it would be with you behind bars."

"Ah, yeah…I remember you having this insane idea that I knew things about Donavon's business," Beth said with a laugh.

"No, it wasn't an idea, I know you do…I just can't prove it is all," Jessica said as she turned to look at Beth. "You got me here, would you like to tell me why?"

"Right down to business. Were you always like that? I'm not sure Luce enjoyed things that way. I mean I know she likes to take her time. She likes a lot of touching and exploring, maybe that's why you couldn't keep her. What do you think?"

"I'm not going to discuss Luce with you. So what else is it you want to talk about?"

"Oh, Luce is gonna be so disappointed, to hear that," Beth said as she walked to the bar. "Oh would you like a drink?"

"No."

"I figured you wouldn't. In fact, I even told Luce you wouldn't try to be friends. But you know Luce, always wanting things her way."

"When did you talk to Luce?" Jessica asked as confusion began to form.

"Oh, she didn't tell you? She's here. I thought maybe it was time for a get-together, the three of us, you know. Maybe clear the air so to speak."

"Where's Luce?" Jessica asked, feeling the beginnings of panic.

"Um, well, she's a little tied up right now, but you'll be able to see her in a little bit," Beth said as she poured some wine.

"Luce…Luce, where are you?" Jessica called out as she started walking to the bedroom. Jessica opened the door and saw Luce tied to the bed. "Oh, my god, Luce are you all right?" she said as she rushed to the side of the bed.

"Of course she is all right, Jessica, but then again it's only a matter of time before that changes," Beth said as she walked into the bedroom with a gun in her hand pointed at Jessica.

"Beth, put the gun down. We can work this all out," Jessica said as she thought of the gun in her purse. There was no way she would be able to get to it without getting shot.

"No, Jessica, we can't work this out at all. You see, Luce here killed Donavon and that…now that's something I just can't let go of. And you…you don't know. I guess, I'm wondering what gives you the right to just walk in and claim to be Luce's family, the right to make decisions for her? Did it ever occur to you that I might just have truly had feelings for her?"

"I was wrong to just walk in and take your place. You're right, I'm sorry," Jessica said as she slowly tried to move closer to Beth.

"You think sorry fixes everything?" Beth said as she brought the gun straight to Jessica's head. "Does sorry bring Donavon back? No, I don't believe so."

From the bed Luce tried to scream through the tape on her mouth and thrashed against the bed.

Beth swiftly swung the gun toward Luce and fired. Jessica immediately rushed Beth in blind panic. She had no idea if Luce had been hit, but she had to do all she could to stop the blond woman from killing her.

The two women slammed into the dresser, knocking things over as they fought for control of the gun.

Tyler heard the gunshot and immediately drew his own weapon and kicked in the door. He scanned the room and ran to the bedroom, rushing in just in time to see Jessica land on the floor and Beth taking aim at her. His instincts took over and he pointed his Sig and shot. His bullet hit the blonde in the side, went through her rib cage and hit the heart. Beth crumpled and fell.

"Jesus Christ, what the fuck just happened?" Tyler said as he reached for his phone and dialed 911. "Yeah, this is Special Agent Tyler, I need officers, an ambulance, and the coroner at the Broadmoor, Room 337."

Jessica got up and rushed to the bed, praying she wouldn't find Luce dead. "Luce, oh god, please be okay." She reached the bed and immediately saw blood. She searched Luce and found where the bullet hit, and thanked god that it wasn't life threatening. Her hands went to the tape over Luce's mouth and gently took it off.

"Jesus, I thought we were dead," Luce said. "Can you get my hands and feet please?"

"Do either of you want to tell me what the hell you were doing here with a person of interest who is being looked for by every federal agent in the United States?" Tyler said, one hand on his hip and the other rubbing the back of his neck.

"Can I tell you after I have this little scratch looked at it? Fucker hurts like hell," Luce said as she went to sit up, winced at the pain, and broke out into a thin sheen of sweat.

"Jesus, Velazquez, I'm starting to think you don't want to work anymore," Tyler said.

"Nah, I love work. But I gotta have some way of getting Jess's attention, and getting shot seems to work," Luce joked as she held her hand tightly against the wound.

Chapter Twenty-One

Once Luce's wound had been taken care of she found her way back to the hotel room. Police were still processing the scene; she flashed her badge, gained entrance and found both Tyler and Sullivan in the bedroom. The two stood at the foot of the bed, which was covered with what looked like ten or so notebooks. "What's going on?" she asked as she approached.

"We found these in a suitcase. Diaries or journals, whatever you want to call 'em, all providing a glimpse into Vargas's organization," Tyler said as he flipped the page he'd been reading.

Jessica looked at Luce. "I'm sorry. Everything here says she knew more about the business than we originally thought."

Luce nodded as she took a deep breath. So Jess was right, Beth had just been toying with me. Jesus, what else am I gonna hear? That she planned that judge's death? "I see. Is there anything about Joe's death?"

"Nothing that we've found so far," Jessica said. "How do you feel? You look pale."

"I'm fine, like I said, it's just a scratch."

"Jesus Christ, Sullivan, we have a shitload of names, dirty agents, politicians, hit men…these will bring down the rest of the organization and put a lot of bad people behind bars."

Luce was about to speak when they heard the ringing of a cell phone. Jessica looked at the nightstand, it sounded like it was coming from there. She opened the drawer with her gloved hand, and on the third ring she answered.

"Beth, my angel, where are you?" Estes said quickly, not realizing the voice did not belong to the blond woman.

"Could I ask who this is?" Jessica said.

"Who is this?" Estes replied, becoming suspicious.

"SAC Sullivan and you are?"

"Carlos. Has something happened to Beth? Is that why you're answering her phone?" he asked even as his blood began to boil.

"Are you family?" Jessica asked only to have the line go dead. "That was odd."

"I take it they didn't want to talk?" Luce said as a frown creased her forehead.

"Yeah, all I got was that his name is Carlos. Tyler, have you come across that name in any of those damned notebooks?"

"Not that I've found so far."

"Okay then, let's run this number and see what we come back with."

†

Carlos paced the length of the floor of his private jet. In his heart he knew there wasn't any reason for someone other than Beth to be answering her cell phone. He hadn't heard from her since he left her earlier that day, and this only added to his worry. It also signaled his time to fly the hell out of here. He walked back to his seat and pressed the intercom button, which connected him immediately to the pilot. "It's time." He buckled in, knowing in a few minutes he would be in the air headed back home. He stared out the window as all his thoughts landed on one thing: he would never see his beautiful Beth again. "I will make them all pay, *mi amore.*" He whispered as the jet began to move.

Chapter Twenty-Two

Finally, after what felt like days, Jessica found herself alone with Luce for a few minutes. "Are you sure you're all right?" she asked as she quickly moved to the tall, dark-haired woman. Her voice was shaky and her hand trembled as she reached out to touch Luce.

"Yeah, my side is a little tender, and I'm mad as hell at myself for giving Beth the opportunity to knock me out and…I didn't realize she would call you too. God, she could have killed us both," Luce said as she looked into Jessica's eyes.

"She didn't, though," Jessica replied. "But I have to tell you, I think I lost twenty years off my life when I saw you tied to the bed and I heard the gunshot."

Luce's arms wrapped around Jessica as she tenderly dropped a kiss on her forehead. "I know. I felt the same when I saw her pointing the gun at your head. I think we've done all we can here tonight. Come home with me."

"I don't think I ever want to let you out of my sight again, so, yeah, I'm going home with you. We can send someone to take your car home or to the office."

"I can drive. But, no, I agree with you, we can have someone drop my car at the house," Luce replied.

"Okay, let's see if the police or Tyler need anything else from us," Jessica said as she pulled herself together and tried to regain her professional persona.

Jessica and Luce walked out of the room in search of Tyler. The three spoke for a few minutes, Tyler assuring them that he would personally take care of transporting the journals back to the office, and then they walked out to Jessica's car.

Once in car, Jessica found Luce's hand and refused to let it got unless she absolutely had to. She pulled up into Luce's driveway and turned the ignition off, opened the door and met Luce at the front of her car. Their hands once again touched and they were frozen in time for a moment. Each fully aware of their feelings in that moment and the fear they had experienced earlier that day. Luce gently tugged at Jessica's hand and together they walked to the front door. With her keys in hand she unlocked the door and stepped aside to let Jessica in. Walking in behind her, Luce closed the door tossed the keys on the entryway table.

"God, I need a drink," Jessica said as she walked toward the small liquor cabinet that sat in the corner of the living room. She had a glass and bottle pulled out by the time Luce had her hand on Jessica's shoulder and was turning her to face her.

Jessica brought her hands up to Luce's chest seconds before Luce's mouth descended on hers. Jessica's fingers grabbed at Luce's shirt, clenching it tightly in her fists.

"God, I've missed you."

"I've missed you too," Jessica said softly. "Jesus, Luce, I thought I'd lost you again."

"I nearly had a heart attack when I saw Beth holding the gun at your head," Luce replied as she held Jessica close.

"Are you sure you're all right?" Jessica asked as she pulled far enough away from Luce to look into the deep blue eyes.

"Yes, baby, the doctor wouldn't have let me leave if it had been anything bad. The bullet just grazed my side."

Loosening her grip on Luce's shirt Jessica's fingers began to undo the buttons, dropping kisses on the flesh that was slowly revealed. She was rewarded with a soft moan that escaped Luce's lips and a deep intake of breath.

With her voice growing husky with each button that was undone, Luce said, "Not here," and led Jessica to her bedroom.

Once in the bedroom Jessica's eyes dropped to the stark white gauze bandage taped to Luce's left side.

Luce reached out and tenderly lifted Jessica's face up so that she could see straight into the amazingly blue eyes, "I'm fine, sweetheart, I promise," she said before dropping her mouth down for another kiss. Luce's hand wrapped around Jessica's head and one kiss became two, each one hungrier than the last as the fire began to build.

"Make love to me, Luce, I need you," Jessica said, almost pleading.

"God, I want to Jess, but…"

"Luce, stop talking," Jessica said as her trembling hand moved up Luce's toned side. Her fingers skipping over the bandage and up Luce's ribs as she gently placed her lips on Luce's.

Luce lost the control she had been trying to hang on to and gave in to her desire. She groaned as she deepened the kiss. Her hands and fingers began to pull at clothing and pushed them toward the bed. Jessica felt a trail of fire everywhere Luce's mouth and fingers touched. She wanted more, she wanted Luce and she wanted her now. "Luce, please, I need you," she said breathlessly.

Luce responded by pushing Jessica down on the bed and lowering herself over her, her lips finding and kissing the spot on Jessica's neck that pulsed before she began nibbling and gently sucking at it. Luce's fingertips brushed over Jessica's hardening nipples even as she felt Jessica's growing wetness on her knee situated between Jessica's legs.

✝

Hours later as they lay in each other's arms, Jessica listened to the rhythmic breathing coming from Luce. She let the tear slide down her face as she thought of how close she had come to never being in this woman's arms again. She thanked God that Luce had survived both gunshot wounds, and that Luce had found it in her heart to give her another chance. "I won't leave you again, Luce, I promise," she whispered softly into the tall, raven-haired beauty's shoulder.

†

In the weeks that followed Beth's shooting, Jessica and Luce were busy tying up loose ends. Jessica had formally wrapped up her investigation into the leaks in the department with Tyler. There were internal hearings all three had to deal with over Beth Ryan's death, and there were plenty of journals to go through from Beth's belongings. Through the journals they were given the identity of the "Chameleon." Carlos Estes, according to the entries, was Donavon's half-brother, and, if possible, more ruthless that Vargas himself. Beth had clearly played both brothers. She led Estes to believe there would be more to their relationship. From what could be surmised, she had used him to escape custody and planned to use all the information from Vargas's contacts to become the new head of the organization.

As it turned out Beth did have quite a bit of information on Vargas's organization along with lists of hit men, and contracts that had been put out. One of them included the hit on Judge Marcus Stone. That along with the coin, which had been found in Beth's personal effects at the hotel, was all that was needed to tie her to his death. Whether she was directly involved or not, she knew about it, which at the very least made her an accomplice.

Luce met with Amanda and gave her the exclusive she had promised, leaving out what she needed to but giving enough to satisfy Amanda and her bosses.

Now all that remained was to decide where the two federal agents went from here. Luce knew she wanted to be with Jessica, that the woman had her heart. She just wasn't a hundred percent sure Jess felt the same way. Sure, she had admitted that she was tired of coming home to an empty apartment but she didn't say she wanted to come home to her.

So here she was, with the radio playing in the background, pacing the floor as she waited for Jess to arrive. Once she heard the crunching of the gravel in her driveway, Luce bolted to the door and eagerly waited for her to get out of the vehicle.

Jessica stopped the car and put it into park, shut off the ignition, and opened the door. As she stood, she saw Luce standing at the door, waiting. With her heart skipping a beat, she smiled at the tall, tanned woman. Twice now, she had watched the woman be shot, twice she had faced possibly losing her to death, and twice she had been given another chance to do this right. She walked toward Luce, who began walking toward her. It wasn't long before Jessica dropped her purse and wrapped her arms around Luce, who was wrapping her arms around Jess. Luce dropped her mouth to Jessica's and felt the softest, sweetest lips part beneath hers. Pulling away briefly she whispered, "Please tell me you'll never leave me again."

"Never, my love," Jessica answered as she heard the words drifting from the radio...the words she knew in her heart to be true. She knew she would always stand by Luce, no matter what life brought.

About the Author

Dannie Marsden

Let me introduce myself, I am Dannie, a butch-identified writer. I am committed to a beautiful woman who did me the honor of becoming my wife last fall. We have three wonderful children and one adorable granddaughter.

I started writing about ten years ago and, of course, my stories are centered on—what else—beautiful lesbian women. I try to write about strong women with vulnerabilities and soft, caring women who complement, understand, and support them. I hope I convey the many levels women possess and the beauty of each level.

Other Books from Affinity eBook Press

Dress Blues—Dannie Marsden (Free eBook)
This is the prologue to the Luce Velazquez Learning to Live Again Series

Lucinda (Luce) Velazquez had it all; a job she loved, a woman she loved, and a bright future ahead of her. In a flash of light surrounded by the sound of twisting metal, her life changes dramatically. Her inability to share her deepest thoughts and fears threaten all that she holds dear. Can she allow her lover and others in or will she lose it all?

Deset Heat—Dannie Marsden
First in the Luce Velazquez Learning to Live Series
For Luce Velazquez, an undercover policewoman, her life is in shambles. Her long time lover left her and an automobile accident that resulted in a child's death haunts her.

She has spent the last year proving herself to Donavon Vargas, a crime boss who demands loyalty and respect. Donavan hires Luce to be the bodyguard for his girlfriend, Beth. That causes Luce to walk a tightrope between attraction for Beth and her ability to perform her job for the police.

Beth Ryan, long- time lover of Vargas, knows all his dirty secrets. She and Luce begin an affair that has far-reaching consequences for both of them when Joe Alverez, a man with a secret, becomes embroiled in the triangle.

Love and betrayal become a matter of everyday life. Will everything go up in smoke with the desert heat or can they survive with their lives and hearts intact?

McKee—A.C. Henley
Private Investigator Quinlan McKee has returned to Los Angeles after a three-year absence, only to find herself embroiled in a world of child slavery and police corruption.

Requiem—JM Dragon & Erin O'Reilly
In the final book of the When Hell Meets Heaven Series, Olivia and Amelia reluctantly join forces with Parker and Remington to save their lives and those of the ones they love. The only problem—will three alpha females and an ex-nun be able to work toward a common goal and not kill each other before they complete their mission.

The four women are up against the formidable strength of DOCO along with a corrupt politician, bent on mass destruction.

Can they complete their mission knowing that a requiem will be the harbinger of their end should they fail.

Bayou Justice—Ali Spooner
Hell hath no fury like a woman scorned. When Kara, Sasha's, new lover is taken hostage as a diversionary tactic to allow the drug dealing Bellfontaine brothers to escape justice, Sasha springs into action.

Kara is released physically unharmed, however, her emotions, and budding career in the District Attorney's office are left in shambles when she is held blame for their release,

Appalled, by the failure of the criminal justice system, Sasha exacts her own brand of justice for the acts committed against her lover. From the Bayou's of Louisiana to the jungles of South America,

Sasha plots her revenge.

An Affair of Love—S. Anne Gardner
From a dark past, a forbidden love, a secret comes.
Among the confusion and the chaos of an unwanted reality, two women find something they neither want nor can deny.

In Name Only—JM Dragon—Sequel to The Fix-it Girl
Can an agreement forged out of necessity actually work?

Finding Her Way—Riley Jefferson
Is it love or just great sex?

After ending an abusive marriage, Jerrica Kerrison is finally alive and she's apologizing for nothing! She has a job with a financial firm in Boston, a townhouse in Newburyport, and a sports car she drives way too fast. Jerrica has everything except that indefinable emotion called love.

Madison Jeffrey is a lost soul. A PR job in the south has always protected Madison from the pressures of her family. But one day, fate brings her back to New England, forcing Madison to face her long buried demons, and a sister who despises her.

When a chance meeting brings Jerrica and Madison's separate worlds crashing together, the attraction is instantaneous. After one passionate night together, Jerrica retreats into the safety of her world, leaving Madison to figure out what happened.

Will Jerrica open up her heart to the idea of love? Can Madison finally believe that she is worthy of unconditional love? Or will a devil hiding in the shadows tear them apart?

Rapture: Sins of the Sinners—A. C. Henley & Fran Heckrotte
A serial killer is targeting young lesbians throughout the state of Texas.Texas Ranger Cochetta Lovejoy is assigned to the case. Convinced she knows who is committing the murders, Ranger Lovejoy is willing to do whatever it takes to put the perpetrator behind bars--even if it means stretching the limits of the law by manipulating the judicial system.

Detective Agnes Kelly-Elliott is one of Ft. Worth Police Department's finest investigators. When Ranger Lovejoy appears on the crime scene of a recent murder, Agnes fears a dark secret that, if revealed, could destroy her family ties, and end her career.

This is a dark, gritty, graphic tale of desire gone awry, and flawed characters looking for redemption in all the wrong places.

HER—Lisa Ron

Fox has been looking for that one person who will make her feel complete-her perfect match.

Together with her friends, Megan and Tree, Fox continues her quest while dodging exes and clingers, laughing a lot along the way.

When she meets Madeline, she instantly knows that she finds HER.

Madeline has her own problems-notably a domineering husband.

Can Fox win her heart? Can they make a life together?

This story will make you laugh, cry, and hold your breath as the story unfolds.

With the right person love can conquer all.

Letting Go—JM Dragon

Best selling author, JM Dragon once again brings a story that explores the human emotions that failed relationships can bring. Along with the hope of finding a way to let the past go.

A failed relationship puts Stella Hawke's life on the brink of chaos.

When her grandmother falls gravely ill in Ashville, Stella ends her army career to take care of the woman during her last weeks. Little does she know that an old army comrade, socialite Reggie Stockton, whose family owns the local newspaper, also lives in Ashville.

Will she allow herself to accept Reggie's help to turn her life around and let go of the past?

This is a journey where both women re-evaluate what they want out of life.

Will that path lead to happiness or to a parting of the ways?

Out of Retirement—Erica Lawson

Melanie Stokes was a doctor—a very good one, or so she hoped. She was calm and cool under pressure, and very little fazed her. Until…

Caitlin Joseph ran a small retirement home for older women in need. The fact that everyone in the house was gay was a coincidence, although it did cut down the number of women agreeing to live there.

Mel took up an offer to do some relief work for a local community center when their regular doctor was away on holidays. As soon as she arrived at the home she knew something was different about the place. Was it the little old lady chasing the paper boy down the street or the sign saying "Dykes Retirement Home"?

But there was something about the place that also appealed to her. Sure, Caitlin was cute as a button, but it was more the fact that she took very good care of her charges, despite their rather bizarre behavior.

The older women seized the opportunity to introduce a woman into Caitlin's lonely life, using any means possible to keep Mel coming back. Their plans were boosted by the introduction of another woman into the house, who set hearts a fluttering and blood pressure rising. Now if she was a lesbian it would have been perfect…

Denial—Jackie Kennedy
Time spent in Somalia has Doctor Celeste Cameron accustomed to living and working in a war zone. Coming back home to America, Celeste is glad to see the end of the peril she has been in—or so she thinks.

Danger seems to follow Celeste and she finds it in the shape of Amy. What Celeste feels for Amy scares her more than anything she has faced in war zones.

Amy has the same feelings, but is in denial and vows to marry Josh, Celeste's twin brother, no matter what.

When fate brings them together again, will they give in to their mutual attraction or will they once again deny what they feel.

Through the Darkness—Erin O'Reilly
Becca Cameron is a loner—by choice. She lives in a hundred year old farmhouse built by her great grandfather. A tragic accident in her home a year earlier drove away her lover, and Becca tries to

accept what she cannot change and hang on to the belief that love can conquer all.

Chase Hunter, had a meteoric rise in the Eastman Corporation and was, at thirty-four, the youngest vice-president. To Chase, her work was all consuming leaving little time for friends or lovers. There was simply no place in her life for anything but her job.

When Becca and Chase meet at their work place, the attraction is spontaneous. Life begins to look brighter for both women as work takes a second seat to romance.

Unknown to either woman, someone is watching their every move…

Will passion outweigh doubt? Can love conqueror fear?

Galveston 1900: Swept Away—Linda Crist

On September 7-8, 1900, the island of Galveston, Texas, was destroyed by a hurricane, or 'tropical cyclone', as it was called in those days. This story is a fictional account of Mattie and Rachel, two women who lived there, and their lives during the time of the 'great storm'. Forced to flee from her family at a young age, Rachel Travis finds a home and livelihood on the island of Galveston. Independent, friendly, and yet often lonely, only one other person knows the dark secret that haunts her. Madeline "Mattie" Crockett is trapped in a loveless marriage, convinced that her fate is sealed. She never dares to dream of true happiness, until Rachel Travis comes walking into her life.   As emotions come to light, the storm of Mattie's marriage converges with the very real hurricane. Can they survive, and build the life they both dream of?

This second edition of one of Linda Crist's best-loved novels maintains the original story, while incorporating some reader-pleasing passages that were cut from the first edition. As an added bonus, the short story "Something to Celebrate" is included at the end of the novel, detailing further adventures of Rachel and Mattie.

E-Books, Print, Free e-books

Visit our website for more publications available online.

www.affinityebooks.com

Published by Affinity E-Book Press NZ LTD
Canterbury, New Zealand

Registered Company 2517228